LETTERS FROM THE HEART

KAY BEA

Quills & Quartos
PUBLISHING

Edited by Kristi Rawley and Ellen Pickels

Cover Design by Ellen Pickels

Portrait of the Irish novelist Lady Sydney Morgan (née Owenson; 25 December 1781? – 14 April 1859) . circa 1818. Licensed by the Picture Art Collection

ISBN: 978-1-951033-04-0 (ebook) and 978-1-951033-05-7 (paperback)

For my mom, who is the strongest woman I've ever known. I love you.

TABLE OF CONTENTS

AFTER THE BALL

IF ELIZABETH BENNET had given such matters any consideration, she would have thought the death of one's spirit should come with a good deal of noise. At the very least, she thought there should be wailing and weeping—if not thunder or the roar of a fire. She could not have imagined a spirit being relentlessly forced into darkness by something so mundane as the scratch of pen on paper. Elizabeth Bennet may not have known these things, but as Elizabeth Collins watched the countryside grow less and less familiar the further the carriage pressed on towards Kent, she had no doubt of their veracity. She looked resolutely away from the man facing her, mouth open in sleep, and reflected on how it was she found herself bound to a man she would have thought the last in the world she could ever marry.

THREE DAYS after the Netherfield ball, while Jane was mourning the loss of Mr Bingley and Mrs Bennet was still ranting about undutiful children and her promised future amongst the hedgerows, Elizabeth slipped from the house in the early morning hours for a short walk through the gardens. The late-November days had grown too cold for long rambles. She entertained herself with thoughts of encountering Mr Wickham when next she was in Meryton and of the possible ways she might assist Jane. It would be considerably easier, she thought, if her Aunt and Uncle Gardiner had not chosen this year to visit his business partners in the Indies. She also gave free rein to her imagination in considering all the things she might say to Mr Darcy should they happen to meet again. She was in every way convinced he was instrumental in his friend's hasty departure from the neighbourhood.

She returned half an hour later to a house in chaos. Mr Collins, who looked as though his own exit from the home had been interrupted, sat in one corner, managing to look both sombre and smug. Kitty and Lydia were flitting about the parlour. Their eyes were red and swollen, and their faces carried the obvious signs of recent tears. Mary was sitting alone, clutching her Bible, and murmuring to herself while Mrs Bennet's wailing from upstairs could be heard above it all. Elizabeth assumed her elder sister was above stairs with their mother.

Seeing their faithful housekeeper was also unaccounted for, Elizabeth made her way quickly to Mary even as anxiety threatened to overwhelm her. "Mary, what has happened?"

Mary startled and looked up, "Oh, Lizzy! 'Tis Papa!"

Elizabeth struggled to remain calm and pressed, "What, Mary? What is wrong with Papa?"

Kitty noticed her then and exclaimed, "It was the most dreadful thing, Lizzy! The whole house was still abed, and there was a terrible noise!"

Lydia took up the tale, "I am certain I have never been so frightened! There was a horrible thumping sort of noise, and then Mama was screaming for Mrs Hill, and Mrs Hill was shouting, and then even Jane raised her voice a very little! Mama went to her rooms, but Jane sent little Margaret for the apothecary, and when we tried to see the reason for all the commotion, Mrs Hill told us to dress and come downstairs. But we saw him, Lizzy—we saw Papa! He was lying on the floor, and he was very still and pale. Mama said he is dying!"

Before Elizabeth could make a reply, she heard Jane calling out, "Lizzy? Are you returned? Come quickly!"

Elizabeth obeyed with alacrity. On reaching her father's rooms, Elizabeth felt the worry and dread that had been lurking in the darkest corner of her heart begin to take form. It was as Lydia had said except he was no longer on the floor. Her beloved papa lay unmoving in his bed, only his chest rising and falling irregularly giving any indication he still lived. Scarcely sparing a glance for anyone else in the room, Elizabeth rushed to her father's side where she remained until the apothecary arrived.

The news was grave. Mr Bennet had suffered a fit of apoplexy. The possible extent of his recovery was not certain, and the family should begin preparing for the worst. Mrs Bennet collapsed on hearing this report, and she was removed to her rooms where she would remain for above two weeks. The Bennet sisters simply drew closer together and clasped their hands in silent vigil.

But it appeared Mr Collins could be depended upon to offer his advice on the occasion. When the apothecary departed and they were once again a family party, he said, "My dear cousins, how fortunate it is I did not go forth this morning as I had planned. I have already sent a letter to her ladyship explaining that I shall remain in Hertfordshire as is my duty, not only as member of the clergy but also as your cousin and heir to your father's estate. I daresay that, if he were still able to think of such things, he would now regret his actions of two days' past.

But I am a forgiving man and shall overlook his slight to my person."

Elizabeth startled at the mention of Mr Collins's ill-fated proposals to her as well as the refusal she had quickly offered, but before she could reply, Mary spoke. "Perhaps, Mr Collins, we might all engage in silent reflection during this troubling time."

Mr Collins nodded his head gravely and said, "Your devotion does you credit, Miss Mary." He then turned his gaze to Elizabeth. "Let us *all* use this opportunity to reflect on the wisdom of our choices." Elizabeth could tolerate no more and excused herself to sit with her father.

In the first days of Mr Bennet's illness, Longbourn was unnaturally still as the occupants kept vigil and wondered whether each breath their patriarch drew would be his last. He had brief periods of wakefulness: a peculiar languorous consciousness where he neither responded nor moved but was able to partake of small bits of sustenance spooned into his mouth and stare at them all unblinking.

These periods neither improved nor increased in frequency as the days turned to weeks. There was no change for the better in his condition, though each day he grew paler and thinner despite their best efforts to nurse him. The household soon settled into a new rhythm. Jane, Elizabeth, and Mary took it in turns to sit with their father, attend to their mother, and to entertain their younger sisters.

Mr Collins took to reading to them each evening, most often from *Fordyce's Sermons*. He often observed the sisters during the day then selected passages designed to condemn their activities. He took special delight one evening in a passage that, after extolling the particular works of Mr Richardson and the virtues of his character young Clarissa, proclaimed, *"Beside the beautiful productions of that incomparable pen, there seem to me to be very few, in the style of Novel, that you can read with safety, and yet fewer that you can read with advantage. What shall we say of certain books, which we are assured (for we have not read them) are in their nature so shameful, in their tendency so pestiferous, and contain such rank treason against the royalty of Virtue, such horrible violation of all decorum, that she who can bear to peruse them must in her soul be a prostitute, let her reputation in life be what it will."* He looked directly at Elizabeth when he spoke the last words, but she told herself she was above reproof and would not even incline her head in acknowledgement of his ill-conceived chastisement.

KITTY AND LYDIA were far too young to see beyond a few days in the future, and when it became evident their father was going to remain in his state for some time, they grew restless and bored from lack of company and entertainment.

"Oh please, Jane! Please let us go to town! We must purchase some gifts for Christmas, you know!" Lydia appealed to her eldest sister once again. "Besides, the officers are likely to be about. Surely Lizzy is wishing for the company of Mr Wickham!"

"I wish no such thing, Lyddie!" Elizabeth denied.

"Pah! We all know how disappointed you were not to dance with him at the ball, and you've not been able to see him at all since Papa fell ill. Please? Please let us go!" Lydia begged.

"Truly, Jane! We cannot be indoors for even another minute! You must allow us to go!" Kitty added her own plea to the noise.

Jane looked uncertain, and Elizabeth was about to deny their request once again when their mother's voice was heard for the first time since she had taken to her rooms two weeks earlier. "Of course you will go, my darlings. I am of a mind to visit my sister Philips, and you will come with me." She turned her attention then to Mr Collins who looked as though he could not decide whether it would be better to reprimand his outspoken young cousins or condole with their mother. "Mr Collins, would you join us? I believe we have much to speak of."

As if in afterthought she added, "And you as well, Lizzy."

Elizabeth was alarmed and quickly answered, "But we are needed here, Mama, and in any case, I have no wish to journey to town."

"Nonsense, child. Jane and Mary will remain behind. Jane cannot come. Her health is too delicate since the dreadful loss of Mr Bingley, and Mary can have nothing of importance to do in town," Mrs Bennet insisted.

Well used to her mother's slights, Mary scarcely flinched at her dismissal and only said, "I shall be happy to remain with Papa."

"As would I," rejoined Elizabeth.

"Nevertheless, I insist. You will join us, Elizabeth Bennet!" Mrs Bennet demanded shrilly.

Elizabeth graciously conceded defeat, retrieved her winter pelisse, and left with her mother, cousin, and younger sisters. They arrived *en masse* at the Philips's residence. After greeting their aunt and uncle, Kitty and Lydia were dismissed to visit the shops. Elizabeth and Mrs Bennet joined Mrs Philips for tea while Mr Collins disappeared with Mr Philips for above half an hour. Elizabeth's unease at this turn of events could not be understated. Her worst fears were realised when the gentlemen returned and her uncle spoke, saying, "Allow me to be the first to congratulate you on your engagement, Lizzy! Mr Collins will make you a fine husband."

Elizabeth started, coloured, and began to speak several times before finally turning to her mother and saying, "You cannot be serious, Mama! My father has already rejected Mr Collins's suit!"

"You honour your father with your devotion, my dear," Mr Collins soothed as he reached for her hand.

Elizabeth stepped deftly to the side and cried out, "Then you must see that I cannot marry you! After spending so many weeks in the same house, I am more convinced now than I was at the time of your proposal that we cannot make one another happy! We are not suited in the least, Mr Collins!"

"That is enough, Elizabeth Bennet! Your father is not here, and I shall not allow you to run wild as he does. Your uncle has approved the match, the banns are to be read on Sunday next, and you will be married as soon as may be after the New Year."

Elizabeth turned her eyes to her aunt and uncle for support, but found no sympathy there. Instead, her aunt was already helping to set a wedding date whilst her uncle stepped forward, saying, "Think of your family, Lizzy, and what will happen to your mother and sisters should you continue in your selfish refusal. Your aunt and I cannot take them in, and Mr and Mrs Gardiner are away for the next year at least. This is best for all of you." At these words, Elizabeth knew she was defeated.

Once January 7 had been decided upon, her aunt and mother moved to discussing wedding clothes and the details of a wedding breakfast. Elizabeth's smile turned brittle, and she spoke not another word until she was safely in her room at Longbourn.

Elizabeth allowed herself to weep for two days. She wished bitterly that Aunt and Uncle Gardiner were still in London. With them, she might have found some protection. But wishing would not make it so, and Elizabeth knew she could not escape. She accepted the company of her sisters as each of them attempted to console her, though each for a different reason. Jane thought only that Elizabeth would miss her family. "It won't be so terrible, Lizzy. You will be free from Mama and have your own home to manage. Perhaps you will even be a mother soon. You will see, Lizzy."

Kitty was perhaps even less helpful with her offer of, "It is a terrible shame, Lizzy, for you will be removed from all the officers. But do not worry, I shall write every day and tell you all that you have missed!"

Lydia made the same offer as her sister, only adding, "And I am certain Charlotte Lucas will write you as well. Only think, you are to be married before Charlotte, and she is seven years older!"

It was Mary who seemed to sense the truth of the thing: marriage to Mr Collins was no cause for celebration or joy. When Mary came, she simply sat in the window next to Elizabeth and took her hand. They sat in silence for some time before she tried to speak and finally said, *"All shall be well, and all shall be well and all manner of thing shall be well."* Then she squeezed Elizabeth's hand and said, "It has to be, Lizzy. You are the best of us, and I cannot bear to think it will be otherwise." Elizabeth only tipped her head to Mary's shoulder and wept.

She went to her father at night when the rest of the house was asleep and told him of her situation. She begged him to wake, to really wake and be once again himself, not this hollow shell of himself that he had become. He merely opened his eyes and looked at her, seeming to see nothing and comprehend even less and Elizabeth cried again with the knowledge that he could not save her. On the third morning of her self-imposed confinement, Elizabeth rose, dressed for the day, and joined her family walking to church. She sat in silence as the banns were read and accepted the congratulations of her neighbours with grace. To her mother, she spoke not another word, not even on the day she was married.

ON THE MORNING of January 7, 1812, Elizabeth stood in front of Longbourn and looked over her family. Jane stood with silent tears threatening to spill down her face, and Mary looked even more grave than usual while Kitty and Lydia were whispering furiously to one another. Mrs Bennet was fluttering a handkerchief and boasting of her good fortune. Elizabeth turned her gaze to the upper floor of her childhood home and found the window to her father's chambers. Mr Bennet, she knew, lay in his bed, still and unmoving as he had been since that terrible day in November. She swallowed and thought how very much she would miss them all before pulling her beloved Jane into a final, silent embrace.

She then moved to join her husband of a few interminable hours. She resolutely declined to face him and turned deaf ears to her mother's rapturous cries of, "Oh, my dear Mrs Collins! How well that sounds," and "We are saved, and now we have nothing to fear when Mr Bennet leaves us!"

Elizabeth was certain that, if she were to part her lips to speak, she would forever shame her family with the words that would spill forth. She therefore maintained her silence. It was not until she noted that even wild, untameable Lydia now appeared solemn and still, that Elizabeth gave her youngest sister a smile and finally spoke.

"It isn't so terrible, Lyddie. I am only to Kent, and it is certain you will be able to join one of your elder sisters in a visit soon enough."

It was Kitty who encouraged, "And perhaps Papa will recover soon, and then Elizabeth must return so he can know of her marriage!"

Mr Collins was quick to express his own views on the subject, "My dear cousin, the hopefulness of youth does you credit. However, I fear we must acknowledge that it is more likely that, when you next see your sister, it will be when she comes to claim her place as mistress of Longbourn."

This callous reference to Mr Bennet's illness and the implied hope of his demise left the sisters looking stricken. Their mother however was quick to agree, "Indeed, Mr Collins, you have been too kind. We are fortunate to know the future of Longbourn has been secured."

Mary finally spoke, the first time she had done so since before the ceremony, "And it has been done with no inconvenience to yourself and no regard for either our father's wishes or our sister's well-being!" The middle Bennet sister gave a regretful look to Elizabeth and continued, "I shall miss you, sister." She then spun on her heel and fled indoors.

"You must pay Mary no attention, Mrs Collins, for she is jealous of your good fortune!" Mrs Bennet simpered.

To this, Elizabeth could make no reply and so merely nodded. A few minutes more and the carriage began its long journey south. She listened to the inanities of her husband until her most fervent wish was granted and the portly man proved that he could not be silent even in sleep.

REVELATIONS

Christmas 1811
Ashford Lodge, Derbyshire

FITZWILLIAM DARCY HAD BEEN in residence at Ashford Lodge, his uncle's country estate, for three days when his cousin finally sought him out. Darcy had once again ensconced himself in the library, far from any of his relations, and he was busy pretending to read when his cousin Colonel Richard Fitzwilliam intruded on his privacy.

The colonel poured himself a snifter of brandy and settled comfortably into the chair opposite Darcy's in front of the fire. "You do realise we, or at least I, had anticipated your journey to Hertfordshire to result in rather more of an improvement in your disposition. Instead, you have returned in an even more dour mood than when you departed. I've had to reassure Georgiana that your morose brooding has naught to do with her."

Darcy set his book aside and turned to face his cousin, "Nonsense, Richard. I am precisely as I have always been."

"Yes, and I shall soon replace Wellington. Now, tell me what happened in Hertfordshire," the colonel insisted.

"Bingley fell in love," Darcy supplied. Colonel Fitzwilliam did not fail to note the subtle shift in Darcy's posture nor the shadow that crossed his face.

"Your Cambridge friend? The one with roots in trade and the terrible sisters?"

Darcy raised an eyebrow at the reminder of Bingley's roots. "The very one."

"Is he not often in love?" The colonel stretched his legs before him as he awaited an answer.

"More often than is healthy, to be certain," Darcy replied.

"And what has young Bingley's latest affaire de cœur have to do with your present agitation?"

"Very little, I suppose, except that I was once again obliged to intervene before his honour was unwisely engaged."

"If you have saved him from an objectionable match, I should wonder why you are not pleased," the colonel observed. "Though I fail to comprehend why you do not allow him to make his own choice. He is a man grown after all, not a boy in leading strings." There was silence for a moment before the colonel spoke again, "Aha! I know! 'Twas not only Bingley who fell unwisely in love!" Though he meant only to tease, it took naught but a moment for Colonel Fitzwilliam to realise he had inadvertently happened upon the truth of the matter.

"Nonsense, Richard," Darcy denied the accusation, but his cousin and boyhood friend was not deceived.

"Tell me, Darcy, about this creature you do not love," the colonel insisted.

The invitation to describe Elizabeth Bennet was too tempting to withstand. Darcy drew a breath and said, "She is the younger sister to Bingley's newest love. She is kind, thoughtful, and terribly impertinent. Miss Bingley thinks she is possessed of a conceited independence, but I found her to be refreshing, not at all like the simpering daughters of the *ton*. She is, perhaps, too free in giving her opinions, but she most often manages not to give offence. She is also prone to debate simply for the sake of it. She is passionate"—here he thought of her defence of Wickham and was frustrated again—"even when she is mistaken."

Putting aside his anger, he pictured her face that night and on the other occasions they had spoken. He continued softly, "She has the most expressive eyes I have ever seen. They dance when she laughs and burn when she is angry." He stopped speaking and turned to gaze into the darkness beyond the library window.

"She seems your ideal match, then. Why are you not in Hertfordshire wooing the lady rather than sitting here with your dusty old relations?"

Darcy shook himself and turned to face his cousin. "Woo her? No. She is entirely unsuitable. 'Tis better that I left the country when I did."

"And what makes this kind, impertinent, passionate woman unsuitable? Is she a servant?"

"Do not be ridiculous!" Darcy snapped in offence.

"A shopkeeper's daughter perhaps or a tavern wench?" the colonel teased his cousin.

"Give me some credit, if you please!"

"The squire's daughter?" Darcy's face darkened at his words, and Colonel Fitzwilliam knew he had come to the point. "That is it then," he continued before Darcy could speak. "You fell in love with the squire's daughter. Her father is at least a gentleman then, so tell me, Darcy, how is she unsuitable?"

"It is not she so much as it is her family! The two eldest sisters were the only decent members of the entire group. Five daughters, all out at once and not a decent dowry between them. A vulgar, grasping, harpy of a mother. An indolent father. And an estate that is entailed to Lady Catherine's parson of all people! That is to say nothing of her mother's relations. An uncle who is a country attorney and another in trade. How could I possibly rejoice in the prospect of relations whose condition in life is so decidedly beneath my own? The match was in every way impossible! I would not have my life made the subject of insipid gossip and speculation!"

The colonel made a rude noise and said, "When did you become Lady Catherine?"

"I beg your pardon?" Darcy asked indignantly.

"You heard me. Good lord, Darcy! *How could I possibly rejoice in the prospect of relations whose condition in life is so decidedly beneath my own?*" he mimicked cruelly. "You've not cared one whit what anyone thinks of your choices before. Why does it matter now?"

"I—" Darcy started, then stopped, and began again. "I must consider Georgiana."

"You have always needed to consider her. Do not use your sister as an excuse for your own arrogance. You have picked a poor time to begin caring for the whims of society. I only hope you were not foolish enough to let your disdain for her family show in your interactions, else you may never repair the damage."

"Why should I wish to?" Darcy asked.

"Because you are in love, my friend, and that should matter." Richard said nothing more on the subject before leaving the room some twenty minutes later.

January 7, 1812
Darcy House, London

Dear Richard,

You will be surprised to know that Georgiana and I have

journeyed to London rather than Derbyshire. There is but little which could persuade me to be in town, particularly at this time of year. You should not take my presence here as in any way acknowledging your advice of Christmas. I will say that, upon reflection, I may have acted with too much haste as regards Bingley and his lady. Therefore, I have decided to persuade Bingley to reopen Netherfield. It should be the work of only a moment as he has spoken of naught but his Miss Bennet these past weeks.

I have not yet decided whether Georgiana will accompany me as I do not care to encourage the presence of certain ladies. Perhaps Miss Bingley will not relish the idea of winter in Hertfordshire. I can only hope her desire for the entertainments of town will outweigh her interest in this affair.

Though I take exception to your characterisation of my disposition of late—a Darcy is never morose and does not brood. I know I have not been myself. I suppose I should thank you for reminding me that this is an odd time to suddenly begin caring for the opinion of society, but I will not give you any such measure of satisfaction.

Your cousin,
Fitzwilliam Darcy

January 14, 1812
Netherfield Park, Hertfordshire

"No, Bingley, we cannot just pop over to visit Longbourn! We are both covered in mud and filth and who knows what else from our journey! At the very least, we must change from our travel clothes! Surely you do not wish Miss Bennet to see you looking as though you pushed your own carriage from the mud?" Darcy spoke even as he handed off his mud-covered outerwear to a servant.

"As I did push my own carriage from the mud, I hardly see why it signifies!" Bingley retorted.

"Bingley," Darcy said with an exasperated sigh, "You did no such thing. You stood in the middle of the road and observed as your driver and I did the pushing."

"Well, I did give him direction," Bingley contended.

"Off with you! Change your clothes so you may call on your Miss Bennet," Darcy insisted even as he considered how to begin making amends to his own Miss Bennet. His cousin's admonishment at Christmas gave him sufficient cause to review his actions when last in the area, and he did so with no small measure of shame. He considered it would take a good deal of effort to convince Miss Elizabeth and her family of his good intentions.

By the time both men were in a fit state to be seen, calling hours had long since passed, and they were obliged to wait until the following morning to call on the ladies of Longbourn. Darcy spent much of the evening in silent reflection. He wondered whether he should have brought Georgiana. Being of an age with the youngest Bennet sisters, she might find them more tolerable than he himself did. That her presence might render him less dour could not be discounted.

January 15, 1812
Longbourn, Hertfordshire

"Jane! Jane! A visitor is come! They are even now coming up the drive," Lydia called out from her place near the parlour window. She had taken to sitting there in recent days, as though staring at the road would bring forth the sister who had so recently departed using that same path.

Jane looked up from her needlework to say, "We are certainly not expecting any visitors. I wonder who it might be."

Kitty leapt up then to join Lydia at the window, "Oh, Jane! I think it is your Mr Bingley, and he has that other man with him —the tall, proud fellow that was always staring at Lizzy!"

Jane scarcely had time to consider her reaction to the news when their mother burst into the room. "Jane! Jane! I knew how it would be! I knew he would come! Now, you must go upstairs and change into your blue gown for it is most fetching and you wish to appear your best!"

Mary chose that moment to add, "If you knew he would come, I wonder that you were so eager to send Elizabeth away."

"What has Lizzy to do with it? Mr Bingley is come for our dear Jane!" Mrs Bennet declared. "It is likely he heard that Lizzy is no longer in the country, and not having to worry about being embarrassed by her wild behaviour, decided to return."

To this, Mary made no reply. She returned her attention to the copy of Fordyce she had been reading and determined to say nothing further until the gentlemen had departed. She had read no more than a few words when Mrs Hill entered the room, "Mr Darcy and Mr Bingley, ma'am."

Darcy allowed Bingley to enter the room first, needing another moment to compose himself before he saw her. His disappointment was severe but fleeting as he saw, almost immediately, that she was not present amongst her sisters in the drawing room.

Mrs Bennet was first to speak to the gentlemen. "Oh, my dear Mr Bingley! I knew you would return. I knew you would not forget your promise. You are quite in my debt for a family dinner. I have not forgotten."

She then turned a cold eye to Mr Darcy and said, "And of course, you may come as well, Mr Darcy."

Darcy observed the slight but replied civilly nevertheless. "I would be honoured, Mrs Bennet. Your generous hospitality is known even to me."

Mrs Bennet blushed and stammered for a moment before recovering herself. "You are too kind, Mr Darcy. It is unfortunate you were not able to join us sooner. Then you might have enjoyed the wedding breakfast."

Darcy could not account for his sudden unease and asked, "Wedding breakfast, Mrs Bennet? I fear I do not have the pleasure of understanding you."

"Yes, yes, but come, sit, for you are just in time for tea." The gentlemen obliged her request, and Mrs Bennet scarcely took time to serve her guests before she continued, "Indeed, I daresay it will be much talked of. You see, Elizabeth is lately married to our own dear Mr Collins! My brother Philips arranged it all. Of course, the wilful girl showed not the least bit of gratitude. But she will be made to see reason, and then she will understand that I have secured the future for us all. And now she is gone, there are no further hindrances to Mr Bingley pursuing my dear Jane. Yes, yes, I knew how it would be."

It was fortunate for Darcy that the others in the room were much occupied with their own pursuits, and therefore paid little attention to his reaction to the unwelcome news. While Darcy grew pale and unnaturally still, Mary resumed her attentions to her book, Kitty and Lydia whispered furiously together, and Jane and Bingley only had eyes for one another.

As Mrs Bennet continued to prattle on regarding her own success where Mr Bennet had failed, Darcy clutched his rapidly cooling teacup as if doing so might save him. The others continued to converse around him, but he was scarcely able to participate. Never had he been more grateful for his reputation as taciturn and withdrawn, for never had he less desire to pretend happiness or even interest in the concerns of others. Only one thought consumed his mind:

I am too late, and all is lost.

January 16, 1812
Netherfield Park, Hertfordshire

Dear Richard,

Your mother and my staff inform me you have decided to stay at Darcy House whilst you await your new orders. You have only yourself to blame if your father's stock of brandy is somewhat diminished. Have a care and do not consume all of mine. It is deuced hard to come by.

We have now been two days at Netherfield. To my relief, the sisters remain in London and it is only Bingley and myself in the house. Though I am sorry to have left Georgiana behind, I cannot regret the relative solitude. I shall not bore you with details of our journey hence. The roads were precisely as one would expect for winter in these parts. Our travels were made somewhat worse by a certain gentleman's insistence on proceeding with the utmost haste. In consequence, we were delayed for a time when the carriage had to be pulled from a particularly muddy bit of road.

Bingley could scarcely wait to call upon his Miss Bennet once we were arrived. The younger sisters are much as they have always been; however, I find I can look on them with more amusement and less mortification than before. They are lively and I find I would not discourage a friendship if Georgiana joins me next month.

Bingley has resumed his attentions to the eldest Miss Bennet. He seems as much in love with her as ever, and I expect they will have an announcement soon. He will have to petition the uncle in Meryton for his lady's hand as Mr Bennet is quite ill. He is expected to recover eventually but for now remains abed and unable to manage his household.

I suspect it will go rather easily for my friend. The uncle appears predisposed to follow the wishes of Mrs Bennet, and she does not oppose the match. He has, in fact, already assisted in the marriage of one daughter. Miss Elizabeth married her cousin Collins, Lady Catherine's parson, and departed for Kent a se'nnight past.

To stay in this place, where every shadow holds a memory of her, is suffering beyond imagining. I wish for nothing more than to flee to the safety of Pemberley.

Your cousin,
Fitzwilliam Darcy

FAMILY CONNEXIONS

February 1, 1812
Hunsford Cottage, Kent

Dear Jane,

I must first apologise for being so long in sending news. My only excuse can be that I have been excessively busy in setting up our home and adjusting to the ways of marriage. This morning, however, my cousin is away and I find myself quite at leisure. I can think of nothing I would like better than to share a cup of tea and pleasant conversation with you, my dearest sister. Alas, as we are much too distant for such an occurrence, I shall settle instead for the poor substitute of pen and paper.

Allow me to start by wishing you joy. I cannot begin to relate to you my pleasure in knowing that Mr Bingley returned and was as much in love as I ever thought him to be. You will know such happiness in your life. Of course, you are released from your promise to visit as I am certain the company of a sister is nothing to that of a lover

Please tell Mr Bingley I am happy to call him brother.

There is so much with which I would like to acquaint you that I hardly know where to begin. I suppose I should first speak of our cousin. I find that he is quite attentive to my every action. I often despair that my natural imperti-nence will lead to unhappiness between us, but he is determined to assist me in becoming a wife fit for his station in life. Little though I hope for success, I shall endeavour to be compliant for the sake of harmony.

Allow me to tell you of my home. It is comfortably situ-ated, and the surrounding park is beautiful. There are enough paths and woods to satisfy even me. I do not walk so much as I would wish. I have been informed it is not becoming for a married lady. Instead, I have begun to learn to draw. It is an appropriate occupation that none can despise, and it gives me a reason to be out of doors. Perhaps I shall send you a sketch for your wedding.

As for the great lady, I must say that her interest in my character is second only to that of my husband, if perhaps less involved. I do think, however, that she is not entirely unhappy with my manners. I believe I have more than once seen a spark of humour in her eyes when she speaks to me. She is a veritable fountain of advice on everything from the floors to the attics, and she has even conde-scended to advise me on how to best manage our servants and plan our menus. There is, I think, nothing beneath her notice.

Do not worry for me, dearest. I am still quite myself. I must leave you here if I am to post this letter today.

Please give all my love and best wishes to my sisters and especially to my father when he is well enough to receive them. Aside from you, it is him I miss the most.

Your affectionate sister,
Elizabeth Collins

⚜

February 2, 1812
Netherfield Park, Hertfordshire

Dear Richard,

I am pleased to learn you will remain on English soil for some time hence. I know you do not find the War Office to be as stimulating as the front, but I have no doubt you will excel in your position. If you find yourself at loose ends, you could always consider your parents' offer. At Christmas, even Hargrove began to speak of his concern should you return to the continent. I shall say no more. You are your own man, and you will surely come to some decision soon. Perhaps the charming Lady Amelia will be of some assistance.

As you see, I remain in Hertfordshire. It is exquisite torture. She is everywhere and nowhere, and I can no more leave now than I could have stayed in November. I see her in each of her sisters, their goodness and liveliness, and especially in their fierce devotion to one another.

While I am overset by females, Bingley is besotted and can see nothing but his dear Miss Bennet. Our party now includes Miss Bingley, Mr and Mrs Hurst, and Georgiana. Once Bingley announced his engagement, his sisters were anxious to return to their brother's side. As the ladies were to join us, I saw no harm in allowing Georgiana and Mrs Annesley to travel with them from town. Georgiana tells me the delights of Hertfordshire are almost enough to earn her forgiveness for my choice in her escort hither. She has pronounced the country charming, and she finds all the company agreeable despite the dire warnings of her travelling companions. She will not hear of departing before the wedding. It appears not even our dear girl is immune to the charms of the Bennet sisters as they managed to have her giggling within moments of being introduced. 'Tis good to see her smile again.

Perhaps you should join me at Netherfield. It is not defending against the bloody French but may require as much intrigue as any intelligence operation. There is scarcely a room that is safe from ribbons, lace, and giggling. I had no idea the gentler sex could be such noisy creatures. Miss Bingley continues in her determination to become the next mistress of Pemberley, and after more than one delicate encounter, I have begun locking my door at night. There are other dangers afoot as well; with Georgiana here, I must take greater caution in calling at Longbourn as a certain member of the militia continues to make himself comfortable there. I do wish Mr Bennet would recover. His daughters are in danger, and their mother will not see it. I begin to think I should have allowed your will to be done after Ramsgate.

Your cousin,
Fitzwilliam Darcy

February 15, 1812
Netherfield Park, Hertfordshire

Dear Richard,

Congratulate Hargrove on his engagement. I have written already, but as he is with Lady Harriet's family, I expect you will see him before he receives my note. I suspect it will not be a long engagement. Lord Haliwell has been trying to marry off his eldest daughter these five years at least, and it appears there is some affection between the couple. As to the request of my last, I naturally understand you cannot take additional leave, and I would not wish to face even a day in Kent outside your company. I require your assistance in deflecting our aunt's continuous hints about uniting Pemberley and Rosings. I believe even Anne grows weary of her mother's blind insistence on a match we neither one desire. Perhaps if I had not fled Hertfordshire in November…but it no longer signifies.

In any event, I do not believe Georgiana will join us this year. She is comfortably ensconced with the Bennet sisters and unlikely to uproot for so trifling a cause as visiting her aunt. I have not yet determined whether I am dreading this visit more than in years past or whether I am anxious to arrive. I do not know how I shall survive Kent, but it must be done. I did not mention before, but Miss Bennet has received a letter from her sister. She relates that Mrs Collins finds our aunt to be quite attentive. If that is all Mrs Collins said, I shall declare her to be the mistress of understatement.

In an attempt to pass the time, I joined Bingley yesterday for a shooting party. I was pleasantly surprised to find myself welcome amongst the group, all of whom were area landowners. When the shooting was finished, we retired to Bingley's study for brandy and cigars. A day spent in company was sufficient for more than a few of the local gentlemen to begin questioning me regarding our friend in the militia and the stories with which he has regaled the neighbourhood. I wonder that I did not set all this to rights sooner. How could I have left these good people to suffer from the proclivities of that man? Of course I spoke nothing of last summer, but I did make it known that he is not a man to be trusted. 'Twas a novel experience to have my word taken not because I am a Darcy of Pemberley but because I was judged an honest fellow after a day of sport.

Mr Bennet continues in his illness. I believe I shall summon Dr. Cartwright. Whatever ails the man seems to be beyond the capabilities of the local apothecary, and I have rarely seen a family in more need of their patriarch than this one. On my previous visit to this country, I thought Mr Bennet to be somewhat indolent in regards to his family, but it would seem I have been once again mistaken. Whatever little influence he held over his wife is now gone and is sorely to be missed.

Despite my effort at impartiality, I find I have no goodwill for the woman. Mrs Bennet has not a single concern for the welfare of her daughters except as players in her games. To one she is indulgent, to another attentive in the extreme, another is no more than an afterthought, and to the last, she is censorious and cruel. Of her married daughter, she speaks only to brag of her own good sense in having both secured the future of Longbourn and rid herself of an ungrateful child. No matter how wretched the mother, I cannot but feel protective of the remaining daughters. To that end, I encourage Georgiana to have them as frequent guests. In this house, even the youngest —whom I believe I have described from my previous visit —begins to display some sense. Wild shrieks and running about have given way to endless giggles, piano duets, and the taking up of drawing pencils. Georgiana is pleased with her new friends, and, to my great surprise, I am scarcely less so.

I confess I have found an additional benefit to the near-constant presence of the lively Bennets. It appears the very suggestion of a pending visit from that family is enough to cause Miss Bingley and Mrs Hurst to develop the headache and remove themselves from company for the day. I find we all manage to bear the slight with good humour.

Your cousin,
Fitzwilliam Darcy

February 17, 1812
Netherfield Park, Hertfordshire

Dear Anne,

I confess myself surprised at the receipt of your letter and can only trust your discretion with my response. I am curious to know more about this Mr Addison. How did you come to meet him, and what are his prospects? I should wish to meet the young man. Perhaps something can be arranged? I cannot fathom how you have managed to keep such a thing from my aunt. She must be very distracted indeed by her efforts to oversee the changes in her parson's living arrangements. I can very well see how you would wish for me to convince her there can never be an understanding between us, but I cannot see how it is to be done. Certainly speaking with her has had no effect. I had hoped...but it does not signify. I shall give the matter due consideration, and perhaps between us, Richard and I shall have a suggestion when we visit at Easter.

I am no less pleased to know you find Mrs Collins to be an amiable neighbour. I daresay the dinner conversation is not dull when she is a guest at your mother's table. You are correct in your belief we are acquainted. I met Mrs Collins, then Miss Bennet, last autumn while visiting a friend who had leased an estate in the area. I know not how intimate she ever was with Wickham, but if she is asking, then certainly tell her the whole of our history with him. Mrs Collins has a strong sense of justice, I believe, and it is likely he won her over with his universally charming manners. I knew she was outraged on his behalf last November, but could not bring myself to disclose what I knew. It is one of many regrets I hold from that time. I am afraid, Cousin, I did not recommend myself well to those in the neighbourhood on my first visit. If Mrs Collins has a low opinion of me, it is due to my own reticence in company. I have been informed by no less a person than the lady's youngest sister that I was thought to be "a proud, distasteful sort of fellow." Miss Lydia shows no restraint in offering her opinions. In many ways, she reminds me of her sister though the younger is not so discreet as the elder. She tells me I am now much improved. I shall accept her words as the compliment for which they were intended.

I plan to depart Hertfordshire for London on March 17. I have some few matters of business to attend, and I wish to call on Hargrove to offer my felicitations. Once there, I shall join Richard, and together we should arrive at Rosings on the twenty-third if the roads are passable. If I thought coming sooner would make any difference to your situation, I would happily do so. As it will not, I must stay with my original plans and ask for your continued patience. I shall do all in my power to promote your happiness.

Your cousin,
Fitzwilliam Darcy

৩৯৩

March 1, 1812
Netherfield Park, Hertfordshire

Dear Richard,

By your convoluted train of logic, one would assume that a second son might never marry—or at least might not be able to marry where he chooses. It is either this or you think Lady Amelia to be a flirt who has accepted your attentions only as a means of diversion by which she might pass the season. Do try to not be quite so ridiculous. I certainly hope you have not expressed such thoughts to your lady; else, she might not be your lady any longer. Bah. Who am I to give advice in these matters?

Had I but spoken sooner, we might even now be celebrating my own betrothal. You would do better to ask your brother. He has made his match and managed to please the family in the process. Do as you will. Only try to recall that a lady's heart is to not to be gained in the same manner as a soldier's obedience. Even I know that much. It is good we soon leave for Kent. You will be able to do far less harm to yourself from there.

I had hoped you might have some advice for Anne's situation. Perhaps between us we can devise a plan. It seems she would very much like to know this Mr Addison better. For my part, I cannot object without knowing him better myself. I shall think on it more before we travel, and I ask that you do the same. At least one of us should find happiness. Since I have lost my chance and you seem determined to ruin yours, we are left with Anne to succeed where we have not.

In Hertfordshire, we continue much as we have these many weeks. I believe Bingley grows tired of one Bennet sister even as his affection for another continues to grow. Miss Mary has proven herself to be a most effective chaperone, and I daresay the couple has enjoyed scarcely a moment's privacy. We shall have to seek someone of her talent when Georgiana is out. Though I still long for the sanctuary of Pemberley, I find myself thinking how empty that place will be. I have grown quite accustomed to the noise and activity of four busy young ladies. Each of the Bennet sisters has discovered some occupation, and Netherfield is frequently filled with their chatter. It happens that Miss Mary does have some talent for the piano, despite her earlier showing to the contrary. She wanted only proper encouragement and some direction.

Miss Catherine is learning to draw, and Miss Lydia seems content to sample both for now. How pleasing it will be to have news of her sisters' well-being to deliver to Mrs Collins.

I hope to also bear news of her father's improvement. Cartwright seems optimistic that a change in treatment will make all the difference to Mr Bennet. Naturally, I am not privy to all the most intimate details of the situation, but I am given to understand that the man had some sort of apoplexy. His recovery has been hindered by a series of colds that have now caused an illness in his chest. He has been made worse by a lack of good air, stress, and numerous other factors. Though it has been only a few days since the changes were made, I have already noted a difference in the Miss Bennets when they speak of their father. There is something less of despair in their manner and tone. We are now all optimistic that Mr Bennet will be able to attend his eldest daughter's wedding, at least, even if he cannot yet escort her down the aisle.

There is another matter of grave importance where the gentleman is involved. Miss Bennet has confided in Bingley of her father's ignorance regarding the marriage of Mr and Mrs Collins. Only Mrs Bennet seems uncon-cerned as to the impact this news might have on her husband's health. She is wilfully blind to the potential consequences of her actions and remains convinced her husband will understand.

Her daughters are not so ignorant as the lady herself appears to be. From what I understand of the story, Mr Bennet first took ill only days following my departure from the area. It was this that kept Mr Collins at Longbourn and renewed his hopes of pursuing Miss Elizabeth. As her husband's health continued to fail, Mrs Bennet became desperate and begged her brother the attorney to act in Mr Bennet's stead and approve the suit of Mr Collins. Thus, the betrothal was effected and the banns read whilst Mr Bennet was yet unable to speak or write on his daughter's behalf. The whole thing was accomplished in a matter of weeks.

Now he has begun asking, in his own manner, after the presence of his second child. Mrs Bennet prattles on as if she has not understood him, and the daughters have been instructed to say their sister is staying in London with friends of their aunt and uncle. 'Tis a sorry mess, and I know not how to be of service to Bingley or the family. Good God, Richard. She was forced by her own mother to marry that obsequious, ill-mannered, simpering, foul-smelling parson! What sort of woman would subject her child to such a fate? Even I, a virtual stranger to this family, could see Miss Elizabeth's evident disdain for her cousin. Was there no one who would protect such a lively and intelligent woman from being bound to the stupidest man in all of the kingdom? I wish to cry out to the heavens against this injustice, and yet I must accept my own fault in it. If I had not run from my heart, she would not be chained to a man she can never respect. How can I face her in Kent knowing that what evil she has found there is my doing?

Your cousin,
Fitzwilliam Darcy

March 16, 1812
Hunsford Cottage, Kent

Dear Jane,

My dear sister, how I wish I could be with you to share in this time of courtship. I believe I would make a very useful chaperone though perhaps not so observant as our sister Mary appears to be. Your happiness fairly leaps from the pages of your letter, and I am glad. I know you will not think me too wicked when I say you must disregard Mama's advice as to the amount of lace on your dress unless, of course, you wish to be covered in so many yards of the same that your Mr Bingley cannot distinguish his bride from the drapes. I know you wish to be an obedient daughter, but please believe me when I say that sometimes obedience is bought with rather too high a price. You know your own preferences, Jane. Choose those that will bring you happiness.

As to my mother's other advice, I fear I can be of no use to you. I believe your experience will be vastly different from mine because there is such love between you and Mr Bingley. I do wish your Aunt Gardiner were available. 'Tis a prodigiously bad time for their trip to the Indies. Perhaps you might overcome your mortification at the subject and seek the counsel of Mrs Brown, who is much closer to you in age and seems very much in love with her husband. That lady, I think, will prove to be a much better resource and certainly less prone to hysterics.

Your news that our father has begun to regain his health brings a lightness to my heart. 'Tis so light, I believe I shall risk my cousin's ire by defying his advice and daring to pray for my father's speedy recovery. Mr Collins is convinced this will only prolong Papa's suffer-ing, but I defer to your intelligence on the matter as you are situated so much closer to the subject than any of us in Kent.

Things here continue much as they have since I first arrived, so I must beg your indulgence when I fail to share significant news.

I remain, your affectionate sister,
Elizabeth Collins

෨෯෯

March 16, 1812
Hunsford Cottage, Kent

Dear Mary,

I cannot begin to express my delight in receiving your letter! Though I sometimes have news from Jane, I often think her tendency always to think well of others colours her view and causes her to see things as better than they really are. From you, I can depend on unvarnished truth. It is for this reason I find great relief in your report of our father's improved health. I cannot be easy with the knowledge that Papa has yet to learn of my marriage. I do hope your mother does not intend to perpetrate her deception much longer. Staying with friends of our aunt and uncle indeed! I must implore you Mary: speak with Jane and this Mr Cartwright. When that man determines our father is well enough to hear the news, you and Jane must be the ones to tell him. I confess I am surprised at

Mr Darcy's summoning of his physician from town. Why would he take such an interest in our family? Perhaps it is a credit to his friendship with our future brother.

I was no less surprised to learn Miss Darcy is also in residence at Netherfield and has been encouraged to know all my sisters. I had rather thought Mr Darcy did not approve of our family. Pray tell me, how did such a thing come to pass? I am most pleased to know you are venturing forth from home more often and that you find Miss Darcy's company to be worth the trial of Miss Bingley's occasional attendance. It can only benefit you to hear fewer of your mother's slights against your person and character. I wish I had not been so wilfully blind to such things before, and I hope you will one day forgive me.

I am given to understand you have been a most diligent chaperone for our sister, and while your concern for her virtue is admirable, might I suggest you allow the couple some few moments alone on occasion? Surely Jane is so good and Bingley so well mannered that neither one would risk her reputation this close to the wedding. Do not roll your eyes at me, Sister. For I well know you are not likely to share my opinion in this. I do not ask that you agree—only that you consider.

I find my life in Kent to be rather different from the one I had imagined. We are very quiet here with only Lady Catherine and Miss de Bourgh for company. My cousin is not inclined to entertain and rarely accepts invitations lest he not be available to his patroness. How she feels about such loyalty is uncertain. Lady Catherine remains a bit of a mystery. Though on first acquaintance she gives the impression of being rather imperious and demanding, if one both watches and listens carefully, there is more than a hint of mirth to be observed. I begin to think she delights in finding those who might see through her façade. Miss de Bourgh is a rather petite lady but seems to be in good health despite her mother's protestations to the contrary. She is a lovely and gracious companion, and I find I quite look forward to her occasional calls and invi-tations.

Oh, Mary, how I miss you! Indeed, I miss all my sisters. Your excellent description of an afternoon at Netherfield left me feeling as if I were in the room. I could see Jane's blush as she whispered with Mr Bingley and hear Lydia's exclamations and Kitty's laughter as well as your own voice attempting to be serious but betraying amusement at their antics. From your description, I shall surely recog-nise Miss Darcy should I ever have the good fortune to meet her. Poor Miss Bingley—how hard it must be to suffer the headache so frequently and miss such delightful company.

I fear I must close if I am to post this letter before my cousin returns. I do love you, Mary, and I shall see you very soon.

Your affectionate sister,
Elizabeth Collins

March 19, 1812
Darcy House, London

Dearest Georgiana,

I am safely arrived in London, and as I told you before I left, I shall remain here for several days. I apologise for departing so very early, but it seemed the only way. You will, I think, be happy to know I have dined with Aunt and Uncle Fitzwilliam as well as Richard and Hargrove. Lady Harriet was also in attendance, and I think I am correct in saying you will like her very much. She is not terribly young, but not nearly so old as to be considered on the shelf. She is perhaps the same height as our aunt and seems amiable enough in her conversation. I am no judge as to whether her heart is engaged, but the match seems agreeable to both parties. I am bid to pass on to you her affectionate thanks for your kind wishes. Our aunt also sends her regards and begs you to reconsider having your season next year. Do not pay her any mind. There is no need for you to have your come out quite so soon as that. I have only done my duty in passing on her words, but they are in no way similar to my own wishes.

I am quite proud of you, dear sister, and perfectly content to remain your nearest connexion for as long as you would like. I am even reconciled to sharing your affec-tions with your new friends in Hertfordshire—so long as I remain your favourite brother.

I believe I shall have some free time on the morrow and shall utilise it to seek out the music you requested. Do not concern yourself that I did not understand your many suggestions of gifts for your new friends. I have made careful note of all your requests and shall attempt to make those purchases with your happiness and approval in mind. I am also of a mind to add to Bingley's library, if only for my own sake. Richard and I shall attend the theatre tomorrow night. There is to be a production of "Twelfth Night," and I find myself desirous of some levity.

I shall send word again from Kent, and I am sure to include some few lines from your cousin.

Your affectionate brother,
Fitzwilliam

March 20, 1812
Darcy House, London

Dear Bingley,

I think I must apologise for the nature of my departure. I know we had discussed my leaving after a morning ride; however, I found the only way to effect a safe exit was to do so while your youngest sister was still in her rooms.

As it has come to that, I shall say now what I intended to say that morning. Miss Bingley is becoming desperate in her attentions, and I have ceased finding any humour in the situation. Really, you must speak with her. For the sake of our friendship, I shall not miss your wedding, but once that is done, I shall have to insist Caroline not be included in any future invitations to either Darcy House or Pemberley. Additionally, if she continues to reside with you after your marriage, I shall necessarily find other lodging whilst visiting.

We leave London in a few days, and I shall remain in Kent until it is time to return for your wedding. If I can be of any service to you or to the Bennets, please direct your requests to me at Rosings. I think I must say: if your request is urgent, you might best ask Georgiana or some other member of the household to write on your behalf. Your script is near impossible to read, especially if you are agitated.

In friendship,
Fitzwilliam Darcy

SEEING ELIZABETH

March 1812, Rosings Park

"Tell me again, Darcy. Why are we calling at the parsonage?" Colonel Fitzwilliam asked as he walked with his cousin along the path from Rosings Park to Hunsford Cottage.

"Because I have been entrusted with letters for Mrs Collins from her sisters, and I bring news of her father that I am certain she will wish to hear," Darcy replied.

"And none of this could wait until our aunt invites her parson and his wife to dinner later in the week?"

Darcy gave his cousin an exasperated glance. "No, Richard, it cannot. I am determined to call on the parsonage today. If you are so opposed to the act, then you are certainly free to remain at Rosings and entertain our aunt. I am certain she will only ask you once or twice per minute where I have gone and when I can be expected to return."

"Really, Darcy, there is no reason to be cruel," the colonel groused. His cousin did not deign to reply.

Several minutes later, Darcy raised his hand to the door of Hunsford Cottage. Hope swelled along with despair as he allowed the knocker to drop, once, twice, thrice. He shifted on his feet and forced a swallow through his suddenly dry mouth. Perhaps Richard was correct; perhaps he should have waited. After all, their slight acquaintance could not account for his calling so soon. Then the door was answered, the cousins were announced, and the time for changing his mind had passed.

THE VISIT DID NOT GO AT ALL as Darcy had hoped and was certainly worse than he had feared. His first reaction on finally seeing the object of his desire after so many long months was utter shock. Elizabeth was, in so many ways, diminished. Her hair was dull, her eyes held no light within them, and not a single impertinent or witty remark crossed her lips. In fact, Mrs Collins could only rarely be induced to speech and then only after casting a worried glance at her husband. Her contributions were largely confined to, "Welcome to our home, Mr Darcy, Colonel Fitzwilliam," or "I am certain my husband is correct, sir."

By contrast, Mr Collins spoke so often and at such volume as to ensure there was little opportunity for anyone else to be heard. When the news of Mr Bennet's improved health was shared, the brief light in Elizabeth's eyes was extinguished almost before Mr Darcy could acknowledge its presence.

Instead, her husband spoke. "It would not do, I think, to promote this false hope. I have seen Mr Bennet myself and can say with certainty that he will not live to see another year. He might even pass before the wedding of his eldest daughter. Of course, should that come to pass, the wedding will have to be delayed, perhaps forever. I do not think it appropriate for a gentleman's daughter to marry a mere tradesman. My sister's services will be required to assist her mother in her time of grief as Mrs Collins will be much occupied with our home."

Darcy thought he saw Elizabeth cringe at her husband's words, but otherwise she gave no indication of disagreeing with his sentiments. The parson concluded his speech with a pointed look in his wife's direction and said, "Do you not agree, dearest?" to which the lady responded quietly, "Of course, you are correct, Mr Collins."

"There, you see, Mr Darcy? Even his daughter knows that Mr Bennet will soon pass and I shall assume my rightful place as master of Longbourn."

Darcy spared a glance for Elizabeth at those words, but her face remained as carefully blank as it had been since their arrival. Colonel Fitzwilliam turned the conversation to other matters. It was not until the parson was called away that Darcy began to speak of the Bennet sisters in Hertfordshire. As he spoke of each sister's newest accomplishments, a shadow of what had once been a brilliant smile ghosted across Elizabeth's face. The expression brought rather more sorrow than relief to his heart. When an excruciating thirty minutes had passed, the gentlemen excused themselves and returned to Rosings Park.

"Your friend seems rather out of spirits, Cousin," the colonel remarked as they walked the lane.

Darcy could only nod his head in agreement. "She is much changed since we last met. I cannot account for her lack of spirit." Nothing more was said, and Darcy hoped rather than believed that Elizabeth would be returned to herself when the couple was next invited to Rosings Park for dinner.

DARCY WAS SITTING with his aunt and cousins in the drawing room when Mr and Mrs Collins were announced. He stood almost too rapidly in his haste to catch sight of sparkling eyes set above a just-concealed smile, but his efforts were for naught. Mr Collins preceded his wife into the room with compliments towards his patroness flowing endlessly from his lips. Darcy ignored the man in favour of observing Elizabeth.

What he saw did not leave him best pleased. Whatever his hopes following their first encounter, it was clear that the only things Mrs Elizabeth Collins shared with Miss Elizabeth Bennet were her name and an abiding devotion to her sisters. Throughout the evening, not a single witty or teasing remark was heard. The woman scarcely spoke beyond making the required civilities, and Darcy considered that he had never thought to encounter anyone less inclined to conversation. Were it not for Mr Collins's continuous corrections and apologies on her behalf, Elizabeth Collins might never have been in the room.

He continued his observations as the parson and his wife joined them at Rosings occasionally for tea and twice more for dinner. Each visit left him more alarmed by the alterations— none for the better—in Elizabeth's spirits. Recalling he had observed Elizabeth's love for walking whilst he was in Hertford- shire, Darcy took to wandering the grounds at different times of the day in hopes of encountering the lady away from her husband. He was desperate to know whether the Elizabeth of his memory dwelt anywhere within the shadow of the woman now living in Kent. His hopes were disappointed. No matter the hour or the direction of his walk, he never saw Elizabeth except when she came with Mr Collins to Rosings Park.

There had been only one notable exception to Elizabeth's silence. Several days into his visit, Mr and Mrs Collins had once again been summoned to tea. Colonel Fitzwilliam had ridden out that morning on an errand for their cousin and so was away from the estate. When the Collinses arrived, Lady Catherine recalled some matter or other she wished to discuss with Mr Collins and drew her parson to the library for a private conver- sation. Anne assumed the duties of hostess and Darcy saw her give Elizabeth a pointed look before saying, "Mrs Collins and I have spoken often of your time in Hertfordshire last autumn, Darcy."

"Is that so? I am sure I was not shown to my best advantage then. I fear I was in a beastly state of mind and did not acquit myself well to the neighbourhood," Darcy replied. Had he not been looking in her direction, Darcy would have missed entirely the fleeting smile that graced Elizabeth's face.

"Perhaps," said she. "We neither of us can claim superior behaviour then."

"Perhaps," Darcy agreed, "but I suspect there is more to this than simply revisiting the past."

"In that you are correct, Cousin. Mrs Collins has told me that a certain gentleman of our acquaintance has joined the militia and finds himself a regular guest at Mrs Bennet's table." Darcy nodded his acknowledgement as Anne spoke. The lady continued, "A table where he finds himself in frequent company with Mrs Collins's sisters—her very young sisters. They are of an age with our dear Georgiana, are they not?"

Darcy felt himself flush with shame. "Ah yes, I believe they are. I cannot say whether he still visits that particular house, but I can assure you I have spoken to others in the neighbourhood regarding his character."

"But you have not been able to speak with my father as of yet," Elizabeth commented.

"I have not. As you know, he was not well enough to receive visitors when I left Hertfordshire." He felt like an errant child being scolded by his nurse.

"I have received a letter from my sister Mary. It seems my father is greatly improved, Mr Darcy. I should thank you for that. I do thank you for that." Elizabeth met his eyes for the first time, and Darcy had to stop the response that first came to mind. He could not say he was thinking only of her.

Instead, he managed a simple, "Your gratitude is unnecessary but appreciated all the same."

"I wonder, Mr Darcy, whether I might impose upon you to ask one other favour. I know I have no right to do so, especially not after all you have already done for my family," Elizabeth's voice was shaking as though it had taken all of the courage she possessed to even speak the words. Darcy noted that Anne had firmly clasped the younger woman's hand in her own.

"You need only ask, and if it is in my power to do what you wish, I shall." He could not keep the emotion from his voice and was rewarded with the nearest to a genuine smile he had seen on her face since arriving in Kent.

"When he is cognisant, speak to my father of Wickham. My mother is a vulgar and foolish woman, and she has not the sense required to guard my sisters. But if my father knows the truth, he will protect them, even from their own mother if necessary."

Faced with the pleading in her eyes, Darcy could only give his promise to speak to Mr Bennet at the first opportunity. Several minutes later, Lady Catherine and Mr Collins rejoined the party, and Elizabeth once again faded from notice.

DARCY WAS REFLECTING on the changes in Elizabeth as he walked out with Fitzwilliam later in the week. That she was greatly altered from the autumn could not be denied, but he had no wish to consider the reasons for her transformation. The colonel finally commented on his cousin's distraction, "You have not spoken ten words together this morning, Darcy. That is uncommon even for you."

"What?" Darcy was startled from his thoughts. "No, I suppose I have not. I was reflecting on the significant changes that can be wrought in a short time."

"You speak of Mrs Collins, I suppose," the colonel observed.

"I do. I cannot say whether Mr Collins is much changed. I met him only briefly and did not care to further the acquaintance though, I confess, I thought him more stupid than cruel. Perhaps I was mistaken."

"Cruel? I have seen nothing of it though I agree he is a rather addle-pated blunderbuss." The colonel laughed at his own humour.

"Laugh if you must, but I am quite serious. Miss Elizabeth Bennet was a wonder," Darcy insisted.

"I shall have to accept your word on the matter. For myself, I cannot see the appeal in such a mousy sort of woman."

Later, Darcy could not account for the feeling of helpless rage that rose at his cousin's remark. He knew only that one moment they were walking together and, the next, his fist connected with his cousin's jaw. They told Lady Catherine her nephew had stumbled over a rock in the road. On hearing this explanation, Anne arched her brow and looked at Darcy, but his face held such a mix of embarrassment and pain that she could not press the matter.

❧

April 1, 1812
Rosings Park, Kent

Dear Georgie,

Richard and I arrived as planned in Kent on March 23. I have no extraordinary tales of our travels to share. The weather was pleasant and the roads clear. We were not set upon by highwaymen, nor did we rescue any fair maidens along the way. I am sorry to disappoint you, but there it is.

I apologise for not sending word upon my arrival; however, you will believe me when I say your aunt has kept us very much engaged and this is my first opportunity to put thoughts to paper. Anne asks me to pass along her greetings and says she hopes you will not be so enraptured of Hertfordshire that you decide to forego Christmas at Ashford Lodge. She has heard much of that country from Mrs Collins, and she declares herself unsurprised to learn the neighbourhood was to your liking.

I have also been given leave to tell you my impressions of a certain Mr Matthias Addison, for whom our cousin has some partiality. Mr Addison is the second son of a gentleman in Staffordshire. They met when Mr Addison was touring Rosings with his sister. After some conversation, introductions were made, and the acquaintance became a friendship over the weeks the Addisons were in Kent. It was not strictly proper, as I have reminded her, but Anne informs me she has not much use for any rule that would place additional restrictions on her already-limited society. Anne seems to find the whole of the affair quite romantic. She somehow contrived for the siblings to visit their relations again whilst Richard and I are at Rosings. Having thus done, it was no difficult matter for her to call on the pair with Richard and me alongside.

Richard and I have since been in company with Mr Addison on two occasions. I find him to be a pleasant gentleman who seems most attentive to our cousin. If the blush on Anne's cheek is any indication, I believe his attentions to be well received. I am now charged with working on our aunt to understand both the futility of a match between Anne and myself and the great benefits of allowing Anne to choose for herself. I would be better served to undertake the task of Atlas. On this matter, our aunt will hear no opinion but her own.

Please tell the Bennet sisters I have been frequently in company with Mrs Collins, and she received their news and greetings with pleasure. She wishes them to know she is greatly anticipating seeing them when Miss Bennet weds next week. She asks after her father's health but says nothing of her mother. I offered to include any letter she wishes to send along with mine; however, Mr Collins did not seem agreeable to the suggestion. He is most attentive to his wife's every move and word. I cannot say I like the man any better now than I did upon first acquaintance, but I shall suffer the husband for the sake of his wife.

Mrs Collins is changed from this past autumn. She appears somewhat thin and is not as likely to offer her opinion as was her wont, but this is perhaps simply the effect of adjusting to her new status.

Our aunt wishes you not to neglect your music in favour of your new friends, no matter how amiable they may be. To be truthful, I am surprised she had no more to say on the subject of your befriending the Bennet ladies. I mean no offence to them or to her, but I do not believe she would have approved of the situation even as recently as Christmas. Perhaps her acquaintance with Mrs Collins is responsible for this change.

Lady Catherine also offers her services should you require her assistance with your come out whenever that occurs, which she believes should happen as soon as it can be arranged—though she reminds me her services would not be required if I would only do my duty and marry. I presume she means I should marry Anne, but as she will not hear my refusal, I simply pretend deafness on the subject. Should Anne and Mr Addison reach an understanding, I believe I shall offer to purchase a licence for them.

We depart Kent on April 6, and after a brief stop in London, I shall arrive at Netherfield the following afternoon. I believe we shall forego the remainder of the season and simply return to Pemberley. I have been too long away from our home, and there are many estate matters that require my presence. It is possible we can return to Hertfordshire in the summer, or you may invite the Bennets to visit us at Pemberley. We can discuss it on my return.

I must close for now. Your aunt requires my presence, and I believe we shall once again be in company with Miss Elizabeth and Mr Collins.

Your affectionate brother,
Fitzwilliam

April 1, 1812
Rosings Park, Kent

Dear Bingley,

These many days in Kent have not passed as I had imagined they would. My aunt, of course, continues in her campaign to see Pemberley and Rosings united. I daresay my cousin Anne grows even wearier of the lady's rantings than I.

There is some little variation in the company when Miss Elizabeth and Mr Collins join us for tea or dinner. Even on those occasions, the conversation is not so lively as I had thought it might be. Marriage seems to have changed Miss Elizabeth. It is odd to one who has spent some time in her company to find the lady all but silent. When we first came into the neighbourhood, I took the liberty of calling on Miss Elizabeth and Mr Collins. As the lady and I had a prior acquaintance, I thought to bring her word of her family and friends in Hertfordshire. Naturally, I began with the news of her father's improvement under the care of Mr Cartwright. I will not trouble you with the inanity of her husband's reply to my interference in the situation; let it suffice to say that Mr Collins did not seem best pleased with this intelligence. Miss Elizabeth was not induced to conversation until I relayed the news of her sisters' improvements and pursuits. Her dolt of a husband had much to say on this subject as well—none of it worth repeating.

On the subject of the Bennet sisters, you need only bear your beloved's guardian sister for a short while longer. Then you and Miss Bennet will be wed, and your days of chaperoned walks quite at an end. How much you will miss the other girls, I cannot say. Georgiana and I plan to travel directly to Pemberley after the wedding, so you are most welcome to stay at Darcy House with your new wife while you are in London. I shall assure my staff see to your every need whilst you are in residence. Not even your sisters would think of such a scheme, and you will therefore be safe from unwanted visitors. On the subject of your sisters, I rather suspect Miss Bingley's new living arrangements will be more to her liking than to Mr Hurst's. If he were more often sober, I would almost pity the man.

I shall arrive at Netherfield the afternoon of April 8. Though I regret missing your engagement ball and, I daresay, even dancing with your new sisters, I cannot but feel relieved at spending less time in the company of Mrs Bennet. I am given to understand Miss Elizabeth and Mr Collins are to arrive April 7. Miss Elizabeth is greatly looking forward to seeing her sisters and father.

Yours in friendship,
Darcy

April 1, 1812
Rosings Park, Kent

Dear Uncle,

I am in great need of your advice. Not since the events of Ramsgate have I felt such acute distress, and to know this situation is, at least in part, of my own making is all the worse. I have been at Rosings these nine days, and each is more unbearable than the last.

Do not be alarmed on account of our family. Indeed, they are all well. Lady Catherine and Anne are in excellent health, and there is news of Anne, which I shall share when I return to London. You might well ask what can have inspired such emotion, and I shall attempt to tell it.

You will remember we spoke at Christmas about a certain young lady from Hertfordshire whom I wished to pursue but had not because of the vast differences in our relative stations in life. Your youngest son soon humbled me on that account, and I determined I would return to the neighbourhood and endeavour to correct my past behaviour in an effort to win the lady's hand. On returning to Hertfordshire, I learnt Miss Bennet had recently wed her cousin who is Lady Catherine's parson. I was, quite naturally I think, dismayed at the news. My unhappiness over the situation and my respect for the lady grew when I came to the knowledge she had not desired the marriage, but rather she had been forced into the situation by her mother.

Now I come to the point. I have chanced to see Miss Bennet, now Mrs Collins, whilst I have been in Kent. She and her husband are frequent dinner guests at Rosings. I previously believed the husband to be merely a stupid sycophant. I have never been so wrong. Uncle, the lady is so altered as to be almost unrecognisable. Richard was so misfortunate as to ask me what it was I found attractive about such a mousy person. I daresay his jaw will heal soon enough. Even my aunt remarked that Mrs Collins is much changed from her first arriving at the parsonage. Her once sparkling eyes are now lifeless and dull. The witty, bold, impertinent woman who captured my heart has all but disappeared and is now but a silent wraith drifting through the shadows. She rarely speaks two words together in company, particularly in the presence of her husband.

I am in equal measures devastated and outraged. I should very much like to inflict upon Mr Collins's person thrice the harm he has done to my Elizabeth. Do not censure me for referring to her as such for it is how I shall always think of her. It was painful to think of her being lost to me forever; it is unbearable to know she is lost to one such as

Mr Collins. I fear all reason has abandoned me, and each scheme I concoct for her protection is more unlikely than the last. She is lawfully bound to the man for life, and I take no comfort in my belief that her life will not be a long one. Tell me, Uncle, what am I to do?

Your nephew,
FD

DISAPPOINTED HOPES

April 7, 1812, Netherfield Park

DARCY WOKE that morning determined to arrive in Hertfordshire in time to join Bingley when he called at Longbourn. Though he suspected the ladies would be much engaged with whatever wedding details still required their attention, he also knew that Bingley would be unlikely to accept a full day outside the company of his beloved and would therefore be fixed at Longbourn every day until the wedding. He had convinced himself that Elizabeth was only missing her family and, perhaps, had been ill when he visited Kent. Thoughts of a much-improved Elizabeth sustained him during the long ride from London, and he found himself arriving at Netherfield with sufficient time to change into something more appropriate for calling hours. In addition to seeing Elizabeth, Darcy hoped to find the Bennet patriarch sufficiently improved for at least a brief conversation. He had made a promise to his Elizabeth, and he would see it done no matter the embarrassment it might cause him.

Bingley made no mention of Elizabeth's being in residence, but Darcy considered his friend was unlikely to know just how much Darcy longed to hear of the lady, and he certainly could not ask. It was for this reason he listened with patience as Bingley enthused over his betrothed and the anticipated joy of the coming days. Darcy found himself growing more and more anxious as they drew closer to Longbourn. When at last they reached the estate, Darcy approached the house with feelings of dread and longing. He would see her again today; perhaps here, amongst her beloved sisters, his Elizabeth would be restored to herself. The sounds of feminine laughter reached his ears, and his heart swelled at the thought of dark eyes once again sparkling with mischief. He quickened his pace, scarcely recalling his manners and waiting to be announced before moving towards the delightful sounds.

When he saw the occupants of the parlour, he had to force the slight smile to remain on his face for fear of offending the ladies therein. He told himself the presence of only Misses Mary, Catherine, and Lydia along with Georgiana and Miss Bennet in no way signified that his Elizabeth was not in Hertfordshire. She might be visiting a neighbour or attending her father. Mrs Bennet greeted him with only slightly less enthusiasm than she showed Bingley. She had finally recalled that she was a mother with three unmarried daughters and he was a single man in possession of a good fortune. He found her sudden approval repulsive, particularly as he considered the fate of her second daughter.

"Brother!" Georgiana cried out on seeing him. She moved quickly from her place amidst the Bennet sisters to greet him. "I have missed you!"

"And I you, Georgie," he said as he kissed her forehead. "Now, what has you ladies all giggling this fine afternoon?" He never received an answer as the question itself set off even more laughter.

It was several minutes later that a question from Lydia shattered the fragile peace of his mind. "Did my sister and her odious husband travel with you?" There was a half-hearted admonishment of "Lydia! That was unkind," from one of the sisters. Miss Bennet, he thought, but was not certain. Lydia simply ignored the reprimand and continued, "We were expecting Lizzy two days ago, but she has not come, and we thought perhaps they delayed their travel."

Mrs Bennet chose that moment to join in, "Of course, it is just like that ungrateful girl to break her poor sister's heart when my Jane has been so looking forward to seeing her after all this time. And not even a note to explain her absence. She has no consideration for my nerves, but I shall not complain."

He ignored Mrs Bennet in favour of replying to her youngest daughter. "No, Miss Lydia, they did not. Your sister and her husband were in Kent when I returned to London. Like you, I believed they were to arrive here yesterday. I said as much in my letter to Bingley." Darcy struggled to keep his composure. Unlike his first return to Hertfordshire, he could not hide his distress behind a display of taciturn incivility. These ladies were no longer strangers to him; they were his dear sister's intimate friends, and ignoring them would be disgraceful.

He was drawn from his introspection with the announcement that Mr Bennet, in fact, had recovered enough to escort his eldest daughter to her wedding. The news was bittersweet. For though he was glad to know the master of Longbourn was returning to health, he could not help but think how pleased Elizabeth would be at hearing the change. That thought took him directly back to considering all the reasons she might have for a late arrival, and none of them were pleasant.

It was not spoken of again, but Elizabeth's absence cast a dark shadow over the otherwise joyful days leading up to and immediately following Jane and Bingley's wedding. The sisters would begin a tale of their childhood only to stop when it came to relating Elizabeth's part in their adventures. Miss Lydia would look almost involuntarily to the window, while Miss Catherine gripped her pen more firmly and Miss Bennet and

Miss Mary exchanged tight glances. For his part, as the hour of the wedding drew closer with no word from Elizabeth, Darcy found he was less and less able to convince himself she had only been ill in Kent. Only Mrs Bennet seemed oblivious to the pain of Elizabeth's absence.

TWO DAYS AFTER THE WEDDING, Darcy and Georgiana made a final call at Longbourn before beginning the journey to Pemberley. While his sister made her farewells to Lydia, Catherine, and Mary, Darcy requested an audience with Mr Bennet. He congratulated himself when he did not scoff at Mrs Bennet's raptures over which of her younger daughters he had chosen to marry. He was admitted to Mr Bennet's book room and found the older man sitting quietly, staring at a miniature of a young girl who could only be Elizabeth.

The silence had just begun to grow uncomfortable when Mr Bennet carefully placed the portrait on his desk and raised his eyes to meet those of his guest. "I am told my family and I owe you a great debt, Mr Darcy. Before she married, Jane informed me that the change in my care and, therefore, the improvement in my condition were due solely to your intervention. I would offer my thanks if only I understood your motivation."

Darcy shifted uncomfortably in his seat. "I can assure you, sir, that my only motive was to see you restored to health for the comfort and well-being of your daughters."

Mr Bennet gave the younger man a piercing look. "Nonsense. You made your opinion of my daughters quite clear when you first visited the neighbourhood."

Darcy could not deny it. "I was wrong. Your daughters are very lively and their manners not fashionable, but they are good girls, all of them, and I had no right to judge otherwise."

Mr Bennet nodded his acceptance and returned his gaze to the miniature on his desk. "Lizzy was always my favourite. Did you know? No, I suppose you would not. When I learnt of your insult at the assembly, I called for my horse and was ready to ride out before she stopped me. She said you were not worth her tears or my anger. I am her father, and I know she was not being entirely truthful. Your words wounded her, no matter that she tried to laugh them away." His eyes never lifted from the image of Elizabeth.

"I should not have spoken them. I did not behave as I should have when I was first in Hertfordshire. I have since tried to be a better man, the man I ought always to have been," Darcy confessed.

Mr Bennet inclined his head in acknowledgement and said, "Then I wish you success. Perhaps you will not wait, as I did. Perhaps you will not fail your sister as I failed my Lizzy. They told me she was visiting friends of her Aunt Gardiner's in London. I knew, of course, it was a lie. But not in my wildest imaginings did I conceive of the truth, and now my Lizzy is bound to a man I know was raised without an ounce of kindness by my illiterate and miserly cousin."

He finally raised his eyes to meet Darcy's. "Still, you owe us nothing. You were under no obligation to return or to offer your assistance. So why are you come, Mr Darcy?"

"I made her a promise, Mr Bennet, and I mean to keep it," Darcy answered solemnly.

April 21, 1812
Hunsford Cottage, Kent

My Dear Mrs Bingley,

How well that sounds! Please forgive me, dear one, for not being in attendance at your wedding. My heart was truly broken, and I thought of little else that day. I fear a slight accident prevented my being able to travel. You will think me a goose, and a clumsy goose at that, when I tell you that the very morning we were to depart I stumbled over the hem of my gown, fell down the stairs, and struck my head on a table. I did not wake for a full day. Do not trouble yourself—for I am now much improved—only I could not travel for many days after.

Of course, you are aware that my brother's friend visited his aunt for some weeks prior to your wedding. I confess that, at first, I did not look forward to his visit with much happiness. Do not fear, Sister, for it was unhappiness purely of my own making. Having now spent no small amount of time with his esteemed aunt and cousin, I had begun to believe I badly misjudged his character when he was in Hertfordshire last year. You know how capable I deemed myself in sketching the characters of those around me, so you will also know how little I appreciated discovering my own errors in that regard. Will it please you, dearest Jane, to know that I have mended my thoughts and now consider him to be almost as amiable as my new brother? To be certain, Mr Darcy is reticent in company, but I now believe that to be a result of shyness rather than arrogance or pride.

As to that other gentleman, from the militia, let us only say I was greatly deceived in his character. But I shall speak no more on that subject. Mr Darcy assures me he will undertake the task of warning my father. I am much relieved, for although we are of but little fortune, I feel our youngest sister in particular could be in danger from W's attentions.

I know you shall have much less time to write now that you are wed, but should you find yourself in possession of a few moments, please send word of my father's health. I do miss you, dear sister.

With all my love,
Elizabeth Collins

May 10, 1812
Pemberley, Derbyshire

Dear Richard,

We are at last returned to Pemberley, and I find myself able to think clearly for the first time in many months. I do not yet see a path forward, but I begin to suppose one might exist. I believe that at least Georgiana will return to Hertfordshire for some time this summer. Mrs Bingley has invited the pair of us to stay with them at Netherfield. How much this is due to her own wishes and how much to satisfy those of her younger sisters, I cannot know.

My own feelings on the subject are undetermined, but I am certain my sister desires to spend more time with her new friends, and as I know the militia will remove from the area before then, I find I have no serious objections to the scheme. We shall both, of course, travel to town in good time for Hargrove's wedding. Will Lady Amelia be in town? I look forward to meeting this paragon of wisdom and beauty you speak of so incessantly. From your description, I have come to think she must be Aphrodite and Athena in one. Though if she truly possesses the wisdom of Athena, I cannot account for her preference for you. I believe our aunt will also attend; perhaps I shall speak to her concerning her parson and his wife.

I continue to dwell on the situation in Kent. Miss Elizabeth was not in attendance at her sister's wedding, ostensibly due to a mishap at home. I have little doubt as to the nature of that mishap but find myself with no recourse. Even your father assures me there is no possibility of interference. As there is naught I can do at present to change the situation of Miss Elizabeth, I shall instead focus my attentions on her remaining sisters. Perhaps in assisting them, I may bring in some way a measure of happiness to her.

To that end, I have fulfilled my promise of speaking to her father on the subject of Wickham. Mr Bennet is much recovered from his illness and granted an interview based on the information he received from Mrs Bingley regarding my assistance in his care. I had much rather he had not been informed, as I did not wish to appear to purchase his approbation. I need not have concerned myself. Though willing to hear me, the gentleman was not at first inclined to give credit to my words. I fear the unfavourable impression I made in the neighbourhood was nothing to the opinion formed by the man himself when he learnt I had slighted his favourite daughter—a daughter whose absence he continues to mourn. I was forced to lay bare much more of my history with Wickham than I would have liked, but I trust Mr Bennet's discretion with all I have imparted. In the end, he took my warning to heart. Mr Bennet feels he has failed one daughter already, and I believe he will now be even more vigilant in protecting those remaining at home. As to your offer, if you are still inclined to visit with Wickham's superiors, I can only support the notion.

I fear I have been too long at writing this and must close if I am to accomplish half of what I intend to this day.

Your cousin,
Fitzwilliam Darcy

June 1, 1812
Hunsford Cottage, Kent

Dear Papa,

What relief I felt at receiving your letter can only be imagined. I am immensely pleased that you are so far recovered as to once again take up your pen and write to your daughter.

I must beg your forgiveness for taking so long in replying to your thoughtful words. I fear marriage has made me rather clumsy, and just after your letter arrived, I had an unfortunate encounter with some exceedingly hot tea. I fear the burn to my arm left me unable to write for some time. Do not worry, for I have since recovered, and excepting some little scarring, I am entirely myself again.

I think that you would not recognise your daughter, so changed as I am with my marriage. My cousin has succeeded where Mama despaired of all hope, and I am now nearly always a proper lady. Mr Collins is very diligent in correcting my behaviour on those occasions I may forget myself. I am sure Mama will be pleased to hear I have learnt to be silent and demure as is more becoming a clergyman's wife. I have little time for leisure as I find that, with only a very few servants, my days are consumed with assisting in the kitchen and maintaining my home. I have discovered I have a talent for baking, and I find the process of making bread to be quite helpful in settling my mind. Mary will be pleased to know I have even learnt to appreciate the Reverend Fordyce, and when next we meet, I shall be able to quote him nearly as well as she. Fordyce's works are a great favourite of Mr Collins, and he insists upon our reading it together for some time every day.

Though I do not envy you the discord it must have caused, I am pleased with the intelligence that Lydia did not go to Brighton. I fear her youth and lack of discretion could have badly injured more than just her character. As for my other sisters, please tell Kitty I treasure the sketch of Longbourn she sent. I did not know she possessed such talent! I keep it in my chambers where I may see it every morning when I wake. Mr Darcy mentioned Mary's playing is much improved, and as that gentleman only rarely gives a compliment, I must take him at his word and say I long to hear her performance for myself. It may be some time before we visit as Mr Collins is loath to leave his parishioners or his patroness, and he does not think it proper for me to travel outside his company.

I pray daily for your continued recovery.

Your affectionate daughter,
Elizabeth Collins

June 1, 1812
Hunsford Cottage, Kent

Dear Lydia,

I know, sweet sister, that you are very angry at not being allowed to go to Brighton. You are young and beautiful and full of adventure. I have not been an ideal elder sister, but please believe me when I say you are far too young to chance losing your freedom. I could not bear to see you chained for life to a man who cared only for your charms but not for your liveliness of spirit. Mama is wrong, Lydia. You need not be married at so young an age. Please, please, Lyddie, allow Jane to guide you. Our eldest sister will show you how you may be yourself and still attract the kind of man who will truly care for your well-being. I daresay such a man might still be an officer. Though I should caution you that many soldiers would be unlikely to afford to keep a wife in the manner you would prefer, and I do not think I am wrong when I say you would not like to do your own cooking or to ruin your lovely hands in laundering your own clothes. Ask Mrs Hill and I am certain she will show you what is involved. I understand from Jane that Mr Darcy and his sister will visit again over the summer; perhaps renewing your acquaintance with Miss Darcy will make up for the loss of Mrs Forster in some small way.

Love,
Elizabeth Collins

July 10, 1812
Netherfield Park, Hertfordshire

Dear Aunt Catherine,

I must confess to being surprised—not at the receipt of your letter, but rather by the contents therein. I admit to suspecting yet another plea to unite our houses and, based on that, nearly consigned your missive to the flames. My affection for Anne is that of a cousin only, as I hope you will someday accept. All the same, I am now glad I did not take such hasty measures before assuring myself of the contents of your missive.

I thank you for considering our conversation in June. There is, as we are both aware, no legal recourse to be had. Miss Elizabeth is entirely subject to her husband's will. However, as his esteemed patroness, I believe you may have considerably more influence over the matter than might otherwise be supposed. Given that, I find your scheme to likely be successful. You need only emphasise to your parson your great displeasure should your wishes be ignored, and I have no doubt of his compliance. I do not know what assistance I can bring to bear; only tell me what you require and I shall provide it.

Georgiana requests you pass on the regards of her sisters to Miss Elizabeth when you call on her. We have spent these many weeks in Hertfordshire, and the Bennet sisters are frequent visitors to this house. I am bid to ask you inform your neighbour of her sisters' continued improvement and good health. Miss Lydia in particular wishes her sister to know she is now thankful for having remained in Hertfordshire. I presume this refers to some earlier communication between the ladies as I am assured Miss Elizabeth will comprehend the message.

With gratitude,
Fitzwilliam Darcy

࿇

July 15, 1812
Hunsford Cottage, Kent

Dear Jane,

You are to be a mother! I can scarcely believe it. I wish you joy, and I insist on knowing every detail you choose to share on the subject.

Do not worry that I might be envious of your news, for I confess that I am not. Please do not think me so very wicked for rejoicing that I have yet to achieve your current state. I do not believe it is anything to do with me that such an event has not come to pass. For though I know little of the marriage bed, I am certain that a child cannot come about from the manner of my cousin's attentions to my person. I have shocked you, but I cannot apologise, for if I do not confide in you, to whom else may I turn? I shall say no more on the subject excepting this: where I once thought our sister Mary would have made a better match for our cousin, I am now thankful that, of all my sisters, he chose me to be his wife. I would not wish him on any other.

There is so much more I should like to say, but Mr Collins

will return soon, and I must be prepared to welcome him home. Remember me to Papa and my brother and sisters.

Love,
Elizabeth Collins

September 1, 1812
Pemberley, Derbyshire

Dear Bingley,

I wish you joy on the coming addition to your family. I am certain you and Mrs Bingley will be excellent parents. I cannot feign surprise that your youngest sister has determined to ingratiate herself with your wife. I am even less surprised at her motive. A rational person would have long ago released the hope Miss Bingley continues to harbour, and I can only ask you to remind her she will never be included in an invitation to my homes, no matter her connexions. The absence of her appointed rival has not caused my affections or wishes to change.

Georgiana asks that I relay her particular regards to the younger Bennet sisters and assures me she in no way means to slight you and your excellent wife. I think I may rightly credit your new family for the improved confidence my sister displays. I am hopeful the change is of a lasting nature, and I suppose I shall discover more when we are amongst our extended family this Christmas season.

In friendship,

Fitzwilliam Darcy

September 1, 1812
Rosings Park, Kent

Dear Jane,

I fear my last letter gave you rather more distress than joy.
I am sorry to add to your burdens. I can only plead that I
was somewhat out of spirits that day. Since then
something of a most unexpected nature has occurred.
Please do not be alarmed as I believe this change will be of
some benefit.

When I sent your letter, I had not left the parsonage in
some five or six days due to another silly mishap that left
me unfit to be seen outside my home. Apparently, my
absence left Lady Catherine most seriously displeased,
and the great lady condescended to pay a call. In all my
months of marriage, that was the first day she had graced
me with such a visit. She was there only a short time, but
after looking over my person with a most critical eye, she
pronounced there to be no reason I should not return to
Rosings with her that afternoon and wait for my cousin to
join us for dinner that evening. Mr Collins naturally
complied with the wishes of his patroness despite his own
misgivings.

In the course of the afternoon, Lady Catherine bid me to
begin calling on her daughter daily as Miss de Bourgh
expressed a desire to know me better. Knowing my
husband would not favour such an arrangement, I de-

murred. The Lady became so insistent that I was obligated to outright decline with the explanation that Mr Collins could not well spare me so often. Lady Catherine scoffed at this but did not press me further.

I shall not bore you with the details of the evening meal for it is the conversation after that brought so much change. We had not long retired to the drawing room when Lady Catherine remarked that I was much altered since coming to Kent. When Mr Collins attempted to take credit for the improvement in my character, Lady Catherine stopped him before he could complete even one sentence. She informed him she did not think the alteration to be in his favour and that she rather preferred the "witty, if impertinent" bride she first encountered. She then censured my clumsiness, saying she had never met a person so inclined to mishaps and injury as myself. "Mr Collins," said she, "it will not do for your wife to continue sustaining these grievous injuries. She must receive better care."

My husband turned quite pale at her words, yet he could naught but agree. Lady Catherine then informed Mr Collins that my presence would be required at Rosings every day to attend to Miss de Bourgh. Mr Collins thought to disagree, but the Lady was rather insistent and would carry her point over all his objections. Before we departed that night, the arrangements were made.

I am happy to report that there has not been a single mishap since that night. I spend my afternoons with Miss de Bourgh. She is a charming conversationalist, and we have much in common. When she retires for an hour or two to rest, I am at leisure to walk the paths around

Rosings, write letters to my dear family, or even lose myself in the library.

I believe my father would delight in the library at Rosings. From what Miss de Bourgh tells me, Mr Darcy has added to the collection here nearly as faithfully as to his own. It is good to read something other than Fordyce for a change. Only do not tell Mary I said so.

Love,
Elizabeth Collins

October 3, 1812
Rosings Park, Kent

Dear Mary,

Once again, you have given me the gift of a visit home through your excellent letter, and I thank you. I am as anxious to hear you play a duet with Lydia as I am to look upon one of Kitty's drawings. I would not have thought Lyddie to have such interest in playing the pianoforte, but I am rather pleased to know she has found an occupation that does not involve flirting or officers. From all you say, it seems our younger sisters are wholly changed from my memories of them. I think, when at last we are together, it will almost be as though I am meeting strangers. Do not think me maudlin; I simply marvel at their improvement and long to see it for myself.

I am equally pleased to know you passed an enjoyable summer in the company of Miss Darcy. I continue to wonder at your description of Mr Darcy's ease in the company of our father and sisters. To be certain, I found him much altered when he visited in the spring from what I had previously known of him, but to find the alteration to be of a lasting nature is surprising indeed. I cannot account for it.

Dearest, you really must cease comparing yourself with any of your sisters. You are talented and intelligent with a generous spirit and a devotion to your family that must be an inspiration to any who know you. 'Tis true you are not our mother's favourite, but I would not count that as a disadvantage. You know very well that Mama prefers whichever of her daughters might be of the most benefit to her on any day. Never have I enjoyed that lady's approbation as I did in the few weeks of my engagement. Yet now that I have been so long married with no evidence of an heir forthcoming, I am once again out of favour. Such capricious behaviour must not be allowed to govern your opinions.

As for our father, I am quite happy to learn he no longer disparages any of you with his taunts of being the silliest girls in the kingdom. It would seem his illness and the circumstance of my marriage have at last roused him to action. I am sorry; you must not think I blame Papa. I know very well that he was not able to speak on my behalf. His letters reflect his abiding guilt, and I know not how to comfort him.

Though my cousin remains much as he has ever been, I am less often in his company and therefore more often at ease. Please do not think ill of me. Mine is not a happy union, and I must find relief where I can. I have now been attending Miss de Bourgh—Anne—for several months, and I find that I grow more fond of her company with each passing day. Though she is no substitute for my dear sisters, hers is a friendship I have learnt to treasure. Only yesterday, we enjoyed a lovely tour of the park in her little phaeton.

The weather here is turning cool, and the leaves are showing in magnificent glory. As you know, autumn has always been my favourite time of year, and to have a few hours to admire the beauty the season offers was a true delight. I believe you would rather like Anne. She is exceedingly well read and has an abiding love of poetry, particularly that scoundrel Lord Byron. I had not thought her mother would approve of such reading, but it seems I have once again been mistaken in my sketch of another's character. I begin to think I should give up the practice entirely. Do not look so smug, sister. I know you have long believed I put entirely too much faith in my own opinions. I fear I shall have to remind you of Mr Warren, and we both know I was only too right where that gentleman was concerned.

At Lady Catherine's insistence, I have included a small sketch of the meadow where Anne and I stopped for a picnic yesterday while on our tour of the grounds. I must apologise for my amateur skills, but perhaps it is not so terrible that you cannot imagine the beauty of the place.

The day is drawing to a close, and as I must soon return to the parsonage and my cousin, I must say farewell. Please remember me to my sisters and father.

Your affectionate sister,
Elizabeth Collins

November 26, 1812
Pemberley, Derbyshire

Dear Richard,

I can scarce believe it has been only one year since I danced with her at Netherfield. Forgive me; I have attempted to follow your advice and not dwell overmuch on the past, but on this day, I cannot help but think of how different things might have been.

I was enchanted that evening. I can still close my eyes and recall her scent of lavender, contemplate her grace as she danced, and see every expression of her magnificent eyes. They sparkled with merriment as she spoke with her friends, burned with shame when she watched her younger sisters, and flashed with anger when she spoke to me.

Every look spoke of her passion and loyalty, and I was lost. I was terrified and I ran the next day. The day I left was the very day Miss Elizabeth declined Collins's first proposal. Had I been there, I would like to think I would have declared myself immediately. But, perhaps not. I had not yet learnt to be humble or to consider how I might please a woman worthy of being pleased.

Enough. I shall be maudlin no longer. I can give you no excuse to spend Christmastide torturing me. Georgiana and I shall arrive at Ashford Lodge on December 10.

Georgie wishes to have some time with your parents before the arrival of our Kent relations. I have had a letter from Anne; she intends to introduce her mother to Mr Addison whilst we are all together. She has contrived, with the apparent cooperation of your own dear mother, to have Mr Addison and his sister invited for a visit of several days. The Addisons seem to have many friends in the area and, in what I am certain is no coincidence, they will be spending Christmas with a family residing not ten-miles from Ashford. You may wish to bring your sword as it might be required to defend Mr Addison from our aunt. Lady Catherine is an enigma to me. She is very much as she ever was in her fundamental nature: demanding, unyielding, and imperious. Yet, in the matter of Miss Elizabeth, she has been exceedingly useful and has acted with naught but kindness to that lady. It confounds the mind. I shall not question it as I am told that Miss Elizabeth's general condition is much improved. The relief this news brought to that lady's father can only be imagined.

'Tis unfortunate your Lady Amelia cannot join the family party. I suspect her father would be more amenable to the arrangements if you would formalise the nature of your understanding. As you have not spoken to either of them of your intentions, you cannot be truly surprised at her family's reluctance. Perhaps your courage will be found amongst the gifts this year.

Your cousin,
Fitzwilliam Darcy

November 26, 1812
Hunsford Cottage, Kent

Dear Jane,

Was it only one year ago that we danced with our friends at Netherfield? So very much has changed since then. I wonder, if I had not been so hasty to judge Mr Darcy, whether things might have been different. But it is no matter now. I can scarce believe I shall be an aunt in just a short time. You and my brother will make wonderful parents. I do wish Mama would give you some peace. I would suggest you appeal to our father, but after so long a marriage, I do not think he will begin to check her behaviour now.

I was happy to hear from Mary that Lydia is learning to play so well and that Kitty continues to improve in drawing. Indeed, it sounds as though Miss Darcy made quite the impression on our little family in the weeks she was visiting you at Netherfield. Perhaps the newfound peace will have some influence on Mama as well.

Life in Kent continues on rather quietly. Lady Catherine sends her coach daily that I might continue my friendship with Anne. I have been assigned my own rooms at Rosings as there are times when Anne feels she cannot part with me and begs that I remain overnight. Lady Catherine keeps Mr Collins busy with the various needs of the parish. Between his increased responsibilities and my new duties to Anne, it frequently happens that I do not see my husband more than once or twice a week. I find I can well bear the separation.

I confess I dread the coming holiday, for Lady Catherine and Anne will travel to Ashford Lodge for a month complete, and I shall find myself quite desolate without them or my dear family for company. We shall make a very small party, just Mr Collins and myself. Perhaps I should invite some distinguished family of the parish to join us. I shall speak to Lady Catherine first as my cousin will never fail to do her bidding.

Please give my brother and sisters and father my love. As to our mother—and do not think I have ignored your entreaties in this department—I have not yet learnt to forgive her. I do not know that I ever shall. I know you do not approve of that sentiment, but I cannot help myself. Our father was ill, but he was not dying, and she very well knew it. To force me into my present circumstance was unconscionable. Please do not ask me to pardon the woman who has been responsible for ruining all my hopes. I am at last finding some measure of contentment here, but it is not due in any part to that lady.

Wishing you every joy.

Love,
Elizabeth Collins

CHANGES

January 16, 1813
Rosings Park, Kent

Dear Jane,

Congratulations on the birth of your son. I am sure little Charlie will be the most complying child ever known, as well as the most handsome. Truly, I am happy for you. Kitty included a lovely sketch of your little family, and it warms me to see the love radiating from your face. It would seem you were made to be a wife and mother.

Lady Catherine and Anne have returned from their sojourn to Ashford Lodge, and I am glad to be in their company once again. I fear the holidays in Kent were not at all agreeable as I once again found myself the victim of my own lack of caution. It was a painful lesson I am not likely to forget soon.

Mother and daughter were somewhat at odds when they first returned. It seems Anne has a suitor, and it is not her cousin. Lady Catherine, I think, begins to reconcile herself to the probable match. Never before have I heard her speak of anything other than the importance of uniting Rosings and Pemberley through marriage. Since she has begun to see Anne's true contentment, however, she has begun to speak more of the importance of felicity in the marriage state. Am I vain to think that perhaps witnessing almost daily the disastrous results of an unequal marriage has softened her heart towards her daughter?

Love,
Elizabeth Collins

ः

January 16, 1813
Rosings Park, Kent

Dear Papa,

I must thank you again and again for the book of sonnets. How very kind of you to send it to me at Rosings rather than Hunsford Cottage. You are too clever by half. I am sorry not to have sent any presents for you or my sisters. It could not be helped. Kitty's newest sketches of my beloved family enjoy a place of honour in my rooms at Rosings. It is a great comfort to sit in that room surrounded by images of the ones I love whilst I read a book from my excellent father. You do not know the joy you have delivered.

I love you, Papa, and I miss you so very much.

Your affectionate daughter,
Elizabeth Collins

January 27, 1813
Pemberley, Derbyshire

Dear Bingley,

I offer my congratulations on the birth of your son and heir. I am pleased to know Mrs Bingley fared well despite the presence of her mother. It seems you are now more appreciative of the talents of Miss Bennet than you perhaps were during your courtship of her eldest sister. You are correct in your belief that she is due some small token of appreciation, and I shall be more than happy to procure the music you requested.

We passed an eventful holiday at Ashford Lodge. My cousin Anne took the dramatic step of defying her mother and introducing to all our family a young gentleman of her acquaintance. My aunt's strictures against his person, breeding, and position in society were, fortunately, heard only by Anne and myself. I felt I should thank Anne when it was done for going before me in this matter. When my aunt and cousin removed from Ashford, they were still somewhat at odds; however, I believe my aunt was beginning to reconcile herself to the match. In the days before she departed, she spoke increasingly of the responsibility of a parent to see to the happiness of their offspring above their own comfort. I am positive I heard her mention something about "that senseless and selfish woman in Hertfordshire" being no one to emulate. When I asked for a repetition of her thoughts, my aunt merely sniffed in disdain and walked away.

Georgiana and I shall remain at Pemberley until spring when we visit Kent. We neither of us have any desire to be in town. In defiance of her aunts, but to the joy of myself, Georgiana has declined to have her come out this year. As she is not yet out, and I have no desire to be set upon by every matchmaking matron in the city, we are content to remain in the country.

I shall let you return to your wife and child with my best wishes.

In friendship,
Fitzwilliam Darcy

⌘

February 8, 1813
Rosings Park, Kent

Dear Mary,

Our nephew sounds perfectly delightful. How wonderful for you to be able to spend so much time in his company. I am quite certain he does not favour Kitty over you; he is far too young for such things. Perhaps it is only that Kitty —oh, I am sorry, Catherine—spends more of her days at Netherfield than you do at present. I recall that, when Lydia was a baby, she preferred Jane's company above all because Jane spent hours at a time in the nursery. Of course, Mama put a stop to that the first time Lydia sought Jane's attentions over those of her mother.

I am sorry to know your copy of Fordyce has been mislaid as I know it has been a most faithful companion these many years. However, as you are the only one to read it, I do not think it likely you will find the book in the possession of any of your sisters. As it is not available for your use at the moment, you might consider selecting a tome from our father's library. Surely, he is in posses-sion of at least one book that might hold your interest. If you are uncertain where to begin, ask my father for guidance.

Here we are looking forward to spring. The cold winter has kept us too much indoors, and as my cousin has fewer duties to occupy his time in winter, we are rather too much in company with one another. I fear my cousin begins to tire of my daily sojourns to Rosings and will seek to lessen them if he does not find some occupation rather soon. Should that happen, I would dearly miss the company of my friend.

Please write again soon, sister.

With love,
Elizabeth Collins

March 10, 1813
Pemberley, Derbyshire

Dear Bingley,

I, of course, would be happy to assist in your search for an eligible purchase. My only surprise in receiving your request lies in the fact that you have lasted so long at Netherfield. Her pleasant daughters notwithstanding, I am quite certain there are no pleasures of that country that would atone for the frequency of Mrs Bennet's visits to your home.

If it suits your purposes, I should like to invite you and Mrs Bingley to join us at Pemberley in May. The roads should be passable by then, which will ease our travel between various estates. Georgiana and I are to Kent for some weeks at the end of this month, and I believe my sister will invite our cousin Anne to return with us. Your coming in May will prevent the ladies from growing too bored with one another whilst providing me an ally in a house beset by females.

Georgiana will miss the presence of her friends, but she has eloquently expressed her understanding of their inability to travel at this time. For my part, I suspect you are correct that Mrs Bennet has determined, for reasons only she can divine, it is not to her material advantage to allow her daughters to travel. As they are not to see one another for some time, I expect the volume of mail between Pemberley and Longbourn to become such that it may be in my interest to hire a messenger. Already there have been exchanges of music, drawings, and if I am not highly mistaken, a few volumes from my library. I have lately acquired a well-worn copy of Fordyce's Sermons, which I am absolutely certain was not my own purchase. I discovered it hidden upon a little-used shelf. Having just read this last to Georgiana, I am required to insist you do not relay the location of the volume in question to any of the Bennet ladies, most particularly not to

Miss Bennet. I rather thought she favoured Fordyce, but perhaps I am mistaken.

In friendship,
Fitzwilliam Darcy

March 23, 1813
Hunsford Cottage, Kent

Mama,

I have received your letter. On the subject of Lydia's desertion, as I have not had the privilege of seeing my family since I married over a year ago, I do not see how I can be rightly blamed. Furthermore, it is my understanding that, rather than abandoning her mother, she is in fact becoming an accomplished young lady under my sister's watchful eye. This should give you cause to rejoice. Now that she can speak sensibly of something other than fashion and red coats, she will certainly make a better marriage than she ever could have before.

As to that other matter of which you wrote so extensively, I find I must beg you to refrain from offering any further advice on the necessity of providing my cousin with an heir. I cannot imagine how such a private matter is any concern of yours. I assure you, madam, you have done quite enough in regards to my marriage. You would do well to focus your attentions where they are better welcomed than they are here.

Elizabeth Collins

❧

April 1, 1813
Rosings Park, Kent

Dearest Jane,

I am so excited as to scarcely be able to hold my pen. I feel as though I may burst with the effort of containing my pleasure.

I shall keep you in suspense no longer, dear sister. Mr Darcy and Colonel Fitzwilliam arrived in Kent this week for their annual visit, and they brought with them Miss Darcy. She is indeed the sweetest creature imaginable, and I have delighted in coming to know her. But this is not the only source of my happiness. Miss Darcy invited Anne to come to Pemberley when she departs Kent next week with her brother. Lady Catherine has absolutely insisted that I be allowed to join them. She is certain Anne cannot bear to be without my company for so long as she was at Christmas. Lady Catherine thought to come as well, but she feels she must stay to ensure my cousin does not neglect his duties to the parish. Instead, she will send along Anne's companion, Mrs Jenkinson. As you see, there can be no scandal in my accompanying my two dear friends to Derbyshire.

Jane, I know you will think me to be the worst sort of wife imaginable, but I cannot hide anything from you. The very idea of spending even a few weeks away from the constant scrutiny and attention of my cousin brings a lightness to my being such as I have not experienced this past year at least.

Your affectionate sister,
Elizabeth Collins

April 1, 1813
Rosings Park, Kent

Dear Mary,

I have at last met the famed Miss Darcy, and I must say she has met my every expectation. I need not list her admirable qualities since you are well aware of them yourself. She is indeed the most amiable young lady I know, excepting perhaps Jane.

I am sorry you will be missing your friend, and I cannot begin to comprehend the thinking of my mother in not allowing you, Catherine, and Lydia to travel to Pemberley this spring. I would have imagined she would be nearly faint with joy at the thought of her single daughters spending the summer at that great estate. I can only think the change in each of you has left her unsettled, and she does not care for the influence of Miss Darcy and her brother in your lives.

I confess my disappointment is not for you alone but has another, rather selfish, motive. I shall be travelling to Derbyshire with Anne when the Darcys return to Pemberley, and my joy could only have increased in knowing I would see my beloved sisters. I do not know how Lady Catherine contrived to have the invitation origin-ally meant for Anne extended to include myself, but I am most grateful for the opportunity to travel to that part of the country. I must admit I am also curious to see how Mr Darcy behaves in his home where he must be most at ease. As to the extended absence from my cousin—well, I feel on some subjects there cannot be too little said. I daresay I shall be able to bear the separation.

You are never far from my thoughts.

Your loving sister,
Elizabeth Collins

REUNIONS

April 1813, Pemberley

DARCY STOOD ANXIOUSLY on the steps of his ancestral home and watched as the carriages approached. His traitorous heart would not hear that Elizabeth was only coming to visit—that she was not his, that she never would be. Instead, it beat wildly in his chest—a fierce, dancing rhythm that insisted she, at last, was coming home. When the ladies were helped from the carriage, Darcy found himself envious of his younger sister. Youthful exuberance easily excused her as she rushed forward to greet her cousin and new friend. He watched the ladies exchange greetings and found his patience finally rewarded as they moved to go indoors. He bowed deeply over Elizabeth's extended hand saying, "Welcome to Pemberley. I am pleased you are come."

Elizabeth's pale cheeks pinked at his words. "You are too kind, Mr Darcy. I thank you for including me in the invitation."

He did not, could not, give voice to his thoughts. Instead, he replied, "I could not deny the wishes of both my sister and cousin."

"I am sure not. I well know the pain of living with a sister's disappointed hopes," Elizabeth replied, and Darcy thought he heard a teasing note in her voice. The sound gave him hope.

"I can well imagine, and I have only the one sister," Darcy agreed. "I have also met your younger sisters and know them to be very determined creatures." The remark granted him the first of what he hoped would be many smiles.

The second smile was granted when Elizabeth was shown to her rooms. He had placed her in a guest room overlooking his favourite part of the grounds. From her window, she would be able to see the pond, the woods, and any number of walking paths to both. He had followed his housekeeper at a discreet distance when she escorted Elizabeth to her rooms and was gratified by the small, if fleeting, smile that graced her features when she took in the chamber.

April 16, 1813
Pemberley, Derbyshire

Dear Richard,

She is here. She is perhaps too thin, and I cannot like the shadows in her eyes, but she is at Pemberley, and that is the material point. Anne and Miss Elizabeth were due to arrive last week; however, there was some difficulty with Mr Collins, and the ladies were not able to depart as planned. It appears there was some question as to whether Miss Elizabeth would be able to join our cousin, but Mr Collins was loath to go against his patroness and, in the end, Lady Catherine prevailed.

I trust you will not condemn me when I say the mere sight of Miss Elizabeth in my home has left me undone. She is entranced not by the richness of the furnishings or even the size of the house, but rather by the beauty of the grounds. She has already petitioned Georgiana for leave to wander the many paths Pemberley has to offer. It is very nearly everything I have wished for, and my only sadness comes from the knowledge that she must eventually return to Kent. I shall not dwell on such thoughts. Instead, I shall endeavour to see her smile at least once every day, and if I am very lucky, I shall know the joy of hearing her laughter ring throughout these halls.

I am pleased to learn you have decided to accept your father's offer of assistance in purchasing a small estate. It seems the appeal of the War Office cannot compete with the charms of Lady Amelia after all. There is sure to be some property or other that would suit your needs in any of the neighbouring counties. Bingley arrives May 10 to begin his own search. As I am joining him, I am happy to look for any properties that would suit. What say you to Nottinghamshire or York? Only send word and I shall act.

Your cousin,
Fitzwilliam Darcy

ELIZABETH WAS ENCHANTED BY PEMBERLEY; she understood both Caroline Bingley's raptures and Mr Darcy's pride. Though the manor was elegance itself, she found she was most delighted by the expansive library and the miles of walking paths. She had applied to Georgiana almost immediately for the use of both, and her hostess had granted permission with unrestrained delight.

Mr Darcy himself had shown her round the library, pointing out those volumes he thought would most interest her whilst stating she was perfectly free to disregard his choices in favour of her own. She had not been able to conceal the smile that stole across her lips nor could she silence the gentle teasing voice that asked, "Shall we now talk of books, Mr Darcy?"

When she covered her mouth in shock at her own forwardness, a kind hand gently removed it and an even kinder voice replied, "I would by no means suspend any pleasure of yours." And she was quite sure he meant it.

From that day onward, she visited the library at least once every afternoon. In the mornings, she could be found wandering among the roses, through the woods, or very near the pond. Though she sometimes carried a book with her, she was just as likely to return to the house with hair a little too mussed to have been properly covered with her matron's cap and cheeks a little too flushed for casual walking. On those days, she could not help but notice that, while Mr Darcy stared as he always had, she no longer saw condemnation in his eyes.

May 6, 1813
Pemberley, Derbyshire

Dear Papa,

What can I say of Pemberley and my delight in being here? Never have I seen a place for which nature has done more or where natural beauty has been so little counteracted by an awkward taste. The estate itself is nearly ten miles around and is covered by meadows, woodlands, and streams. I wander the paths every day to my heart's content. When the weather does not permit me out of doors, I find I can cheerfully spend an entire day in Pemberley's library. Mr Darcy tells me it is the work of many generations, and I daresay that even you would be satisfied with its offerings. The very air of this place restores my soul.

I spend my days in company with Anne and Georgiana. We do all those little things that occupy a lady's time. Georgiana plays the pianoforte so beautifully that I am almost ashamed to perform in the same room with her, but our host often requests that I play, and as a lady, I can hardly refuse. Perhaps Georgiana's prodigious talent is the reason Lydia wanted to learn and Mary became so determined to improve her own playing. Mr Darcy purchased a new instrument for his sister, and she is gracious to allow my poor fingers to caress its keys.

I had forgotten I was capable of such contentment. The only thing I lack here is my dear family.

Your loving daughter,
Elizabeth Collins

May 1813

ELIZABETH SPENT the morning walking through Pemberley's woods and had only just managed to restore her appearance when Mrs Reynolds tapped lightly on her door.

"Enter," Elizabeth called out.

"Begging your pardon, Mrs Collins, but Mr Darcy and Miss Darcy wish for you to join them in the sitting room."

Elizabeth wondered what they could be about but readily agreed to the request. She took a moment to adjust her cap, scowling at the thing as though it offended her, then moved on light feet to join her friends. On reaching the room, all thought of decorum, all concern for dignity, all manner of pride was forgot. "Jane! Oh, my dearest, dearest, Jane!"

The sisters could not move quickly enough to embrace, and neither gave a moment's concern for the tears they shed. When they finally released one another, Elizabeth was overjoyed to meet her nephew and pronounced him as fine a baby as there ever was. Her delight in seeing her family once again distracted her from seeing the joy in Mr Darcy's face as he observed the reunion.

The sisters were nigh on inseparable after that though they easily brought Georgiana into their company. If he had harboured any concerns for his sister's inclusion, they were laid to rest when Elizabeth simply took both his sister and hers by the arm and drew them outside to join her for a stroll in the gardens while Anne chose to remain indoors.

I have once again made my Elizabeth smile. Darcy observed the two sisters, along with Georgiana, several days later from his study window. Elizabeth held little Charles in her arms, smiling down at the infant and trailing a delicate finger down his soft cheeks. The painful sweetness of it was almost too much to bear, but he did not turn away. He knew not how long he remained in that attitude before he was interrupted by the arrival of his friend.

"I say, Darcy, are we still riding out on the morrow? I had hoped to view several estates whilst we are here," Bingley asked on entering the room.

Darcy forced his attention from the view below, steadied his voice, and replied, "Naturally, Bingley. Come, you can review the agent's findings." Never had he found it more difficult to focus on matters of business than at that moment.

May 15, 1813
Pemberley, Derbyshire

Dear Richard,

I look forward to your visit and am quite sure you will find several of the properties will meet your needs. Your mother took three full pages to express her delight and her hopes that your decision to purchase an estate will soon result in making plans of another kind. If you choose to disappoint your mother on that score, please do give me some notice so I might arrange to be out of the country at the time. Mr and Mrs Bingley have been with us these five days, and in that time, we have visited three estates. Only one was completely unsuitable. Of the other two, either would suffice for your needs.

I must now impose upon you and beg your assistance with another matter. Your mother must cease her attempts at matchmaking on my behalf. I shall not take to wife a woman I do not love, and I shall only ever love one woman. As I cannot have her, I shall not marry. I well recognise the need for Pemberley to have an heir, but to be quite honest I see no harm in allowing the estate to pass to Georgiana's first-born son.

I have worked diligently to fulfil my vow to make Miss Elizabeth smile each day. It is more difficult than it would appear at first. She takes great delight in wandering the grounds, and when the weather does not allow for outdoor activities, she can be found in the library. She also plays duets with Georgiana; 'tis a sound of which I shall never tire.

I believe my greatest successes have occurred in these past few days. First, I arranged a reunion with her most beloved sister. Miss Elizabeth and Mrs Bingley have not been in company since the former was married. Miss Elizabeth's face lit with pure delight upon seeing her sister and nephew. It has been some time since I have felt such satisfaction. My second success was a picnic just yesterday. Our entire party made for the pond and spent a pleasant afternoon engaged in conversation and games. I am not ashamed to confess the lady very nearly defeated me in similes.

Your cousin,
Fitzwilliam Darcy

May 15, 1813
Pemberley, Derbyshire

Dear Papa,

You are very sly to keep from me the secret of Jane's visit. I shall not hide from you that I wept with joy on seeing my beloved sister. How I have longed for her companionship! Anne and Georgiana are quite dear to me, but they are not my Jane.

Jane and Charles arrived only two days after my last letter to you, but I believe they plan to stay for several weeks. Mr Darcy and Charles are very much engaged with the estate, so I see little of them except after dinner. What can I say of your grandson that you do not already know? Little Charlie is an absolute joy. He is a happy baby with an excellent disposition. With his mother's looks and his father's humour, he is destined to be a good man.

Yesterday our entire party—Anne, Georgiana, Charles, Jane, Charlie, Mr Darcy and I—partook of a picnic near the pond. It was truly a perfect day. Mr Darcy saw to the comfort of all his guests. There was nothing that needed to be done that he did not do himself. There was an abundance of excellent food and intelligent conversation. We sat on blankets in the shade of a massive oak and spoke of happy memories. We played a wonderful game of similes, which I am sure you will not be surprised to find Mr Darcy won. Though I shall say I came very close to it in the end.

I have heard from no one in Kent save Lady Catherine. She tells me my cousin is very much engaged with his duties and will not be able to join me any time soon. I took the news quite cheerfully.

I love you, Papa.
Elizabeth Collins

June 21, 1813
Pemberley, Derbyshire

Dear Jane,

It seems wholly unfair, after being deprived of your company for more than a year, to be parted again after so short a reunion. I miss you already, and I am certain Charlie misses his favourite aunt.

It has now been three weeks since you left Pemberley. Have you told Mama yet that you are looking for an estate and will settle in Derbyshire as soon as an eligible purchase presents? I think not, for surely her lamentations would be so loud as to be heard even at this distance.

I write to impart good news. Our dear Anne is to be married. I do not believe it will be a long engagement as each of the parties is anxious to begin a life together. As the groom is a second son, the couple will reside at Rosings. I do not know whether Lady Catherine will retire to the dowager house. It is rather difficult to imagine Rosings without her formidable presence.

Alas, along with the happiness there must be some sorrow. Now that there is a wedding to plan, we must all return to Kent. Dearest Jane, I hope you will not judge me too harshly when I say that I shall leave the very best of me behind at Pemberley. These past months have been like a dream. I have been surrounded by friends. I have been at peace, and I have not known an instant of fear except in the night. We none of us can control our dreams, and that is where my cousin finds me.

But to Kent I must go, and I shall hope that this time apart has brought a change to the one I must call husband. If it has, then perhaps I shall find some measure of contentment in that country.

Your affectionate sister,
Elizabeth Collins

UNHAPPY RETURNS

June 24, 1813
Pemberley, Derbyshire

Dear Richard,

I write at our cousin's bidding as she claims to be too overcome with joy to undertake the task herself. You will recall, for who could not, Anne introduced her mother to a certain gentleman last Christmas. When Anne determined she would travel to Derbyshire, she wrote immediately to Miss Addison. In consequence, Mr Addison and his sister arrived in the neighbourhood just after my last letter. Miss Addison joined the ladies here at Pemberley, but as Mr Addison was courting our cousin, he took a room at the inn in Lambton.

You will note I say he was courting our cousin. Mr Addison, Matthias as he prefers, proposed to our Anne some five days ago and she has accepted him. If my aunt agrees to the scheme, the couple plan to wed in August in Kent.

Anne was not initially in favour of marrying from her home, as she is reluctant to have Mr Collins perform the ceremony. Ultimately, her regard for Miss Elizabeth and desire to have that lady as her witness took precedence. It was decided to be very unlikely Mr Collins would allow his wife to travel again so soon after her return from this county. If you wish, you are welcome to extend your July visit and travel with us to Rosings.

I had forgotten, or perhaps had never noticed, how very quiet are the halls of my home. Miss Addison departed with her brother the day after he proposed to Anne, and our remaining guests made for Kent this morning. It is now only Georgiana, Mrs Annesley, and I in the estate, and the silence echoes loudly around me. My greatest consolation is the knowledge that I shall see Miss Elizabeth again in six weeks' time when we travel for Anne's wedding. Until then, I am content to remember her smile as she played a duet with Georgiana, the gentle music of her voice, and the sunlight in her hair as she wandered through my mother's rose garden or strolled around the lake. Though we naturally could not speak of such a thing, I believe Pemberley had started to work its restorative magic on her and she had begun to heal. Certainly, there were fewer shadows in her eyes, more smiles on her lips, and in her conversation, a greater semblance to the woman of my memory. If all I may have of her are these moments, I am determined it will be enough.

Your cousin,
Fitzwilliam Darcy

July 6, 1813
Rosings Park, Kent

Dear Mary,

I have been returned to Kent these ten days and I find my thoughts are very often turned northward. I hope I do not disappoint you, dear sister, but the weeks I spent in Derbyshire were the happiest I have known since the day of my marriage, and I find I cannot help but dwell on them. I am fortunate that my presence is often required at Rosings to assist with preparations for the wedding, and my cousin finds himself very much engaged with his duties, else I fear he would be most displeased with my distraction.

I am pleased to know you expect the Darcys to be once again at Netherfield in the autumn. Georgiana spoke of all my sisters with great fondness, and I believe she shares your eagerness to visit. Georgiana spoke especially of your talent on the pianoforte and how she enjoyed playing with you. I am afraid I was but a poor substitute though she was very kind not to say so. We are all looking forward to Anne's wedding, which is only weeks away.

You will think me quite ridiculous I am sure, but as we have been sorting through fabrics and patterns for Anne, she has insisted I am to have a new gown. 'Tis a silly thing, I know, but I am quite pleased as it will be the first new gown I have had since my marriage. Though the bride most certainly could have travelled to London for her trousseau, she has insisted on purchasing everything locally. She claims it is a necessary show of good will. Additionally, she said that, as she will soon depart on a journey of some weeks, she does not wish to be parted from my company any more than necessary. I teased that she has been without my presence these many years and she cannot have grown accustomed to me in so little time. She begged to disagree and insisted she was in earnest. I had not the heart to tease any further.

In truth, though I should admit it to none but you, I am rather touched at her attachment. There are few people whom I love and fewer still of whom I think well. Anne is counted among those few.

I must close as we are departing even now for the dress-makers. Hug all of my sisters and my father.

With love,
Elizabeth Collins

August 1, 1813
Pemberley, Derbyshire

Dear Anne,

I commend you, Cousin, for your ability to outmanoeuvre your mother's parson. I had forgotten the bishop is one of your de Bourgh relations. It was very clever of you to enlist your mother's aid in convincing him to perform your wedding ceremony. Not even that obsequious idiot in the parsonage could object to such a scheme. I daresay he finds the situation only right for the—what did he call you?

—Oh, yes, the brightest ornament of the British court.

Richard will soon sell his commission. I believe he has determined at long last to formalise his status with Lady Amelia. To that end, he has found an estate in Nottinghamshire he intends to purchase as soon as may be. As he has been staying here whilst he searched for an estate, he will travel with us to your wedding. Georgiana, Richard, and I plan to arrive on August 14.

I have given considerable thought to an appropriate gift for my once-presumed betrothed as she becomes the wife of another. I cannot give you happiness, for that you have already found. You are in no great need of money or an estate. At last, I determined I would provide your accommodations on your wedding trip. You will recall perhaps that the Darcy family owns a small property in Bath. I have written the staff and instructed them to prepare for your arrival. I know you had planned to stay with various friends and relations on your wedding trip, but I thought a bit of privacy might be more desirable.

Your cousin,
Fitzwilliam Darcy

August 17, 1813
Hunsford Cottage, Kent

Dear Jane,

I wish you joy on the coming addition to your family.

Little Charlie will be an excellent elder brother.

Mr and Mrs Addison have left for their wedding tour. They will travel the country for three weeks before returning to Kent to take up their lives. Mr Addison is a pleasant, cheerful sort of fellow, and he exhibits every possible kindness to his wife and her mother. They will make a merry party. It was not long after they departed that Lady Catherine was called to London. There is apparently some legal matter regarding the estate that can only be resolved in person.

In the absence of both Anne and Lady Catherine, I have returned to Hunsford Cottage. Indeed, once Anne returns, I think it will be difficult to contrive a reason she should need my companionship, and I shall likely spend less time at Rosings than I should like.

My cousin is unchanged from the earliest days of our marriage. Though Lady Catherine endeavours to keep him very much engaged with his duties to the parish, when he is home he continues in his plan to improve my character and, in fact, has redoubled his efforts because of what he terms my relapse in the months of our separation.

I cannot regret my time away, difficult as it is to reconcile myself to my present circumstance. I find that even the memories of my friends at Pemberley bring a certain peace to my mind. I hope, sister, that you treasure your dear Charles. I believe that he and his friend Mr Darcy are the rarest of men, and you are extraordinarily fortunate

in his love for you. Kiss my nephew and give my
regards to my sisters and father.

Your affectionate sister,
Elizabeth Collins

᳇᷅᷄

September 20, 1813
Rosings Park, Kent

Dear Mr Bennet,

Forgive this abrupt introduction. I am Matthias Addison,
husband to the former Anne de Bourgh and newly master
of Rosings Park. I have taken the liberty of writing to you
on your daughter's behalf. At the insistence of my wife
and her mother, and indeed I offered no objection to the
scheme, your daughter has been removed to Rosings
Park. We anticipate her stay with us to be of some duration. I fear, sir, that I have given you cause for some alarm.
I shall not trifle with you; though Mrs Collins is now
recovering, she was in very poor condition when she first
arrived.

Mrs Addison and I had not long returned from our
wedding tour when she observed Mrs Collins had yet to
pay a call. It is my understanding this was quite unusual
as it was their established routine for Mrs Collins to call
daily. As my mother-in-law has also been absent, it was
initially assumed Mrs Collins, perhaps, was allowing
time for the three of us to recover from our travels.
However, when three days had passed with no
word from Mrs Collins, my wife and her mother,

Lady Catherine, set forth immediately to call upon the parsonage.

When they were announced to Mrs Collins, she was able to stand to greet them only with great difficulty. Though she attempted to hide her circumstances, it did not take long for the ladies to determine Mrs Collins was seriously injured indeed. Though she would not speak a word against Mr Collins, the housekeeper and the servants of that house, who have no love for their master, did not scruple to give a full account as to the cause and nature of the injuries to their beloved mistress. The full force of my esteemed mother-in-law's will was brought quickly to bear, and with the assistance of a few trusted servants and a small dose of laudanum, Mrs Collins was bundled into our carriage and brought directly to Rosings. Here she has remained these ten days.

It is the express wish of my family to offer shelter to Mrs Collins for so long as it is needed. While her husband certainly retains the right to claim his wife, it is our belief that he will not do so as long as she resides in the home of his patroness. We did extend an offer to assist your daughter in obtaining an ecclesiastical separation, but she would not hear of anything that might attach scandal to your good family. The story that has been circulated in the village is simply that Mrs Collins has taken ill and requires constant care for her recovery. Her husband's reputation is such that the story has not been questioned, and any censure has been reserved for the gentleman. Our only regret is in not taking this action sooner.

Your daughter had no wish to inform her family of her situation. She is experiencing no small amount of mortification and does not want her family to share in her shame. My wife works diligently to disabuse her of such notions but to no avail. It is for this reason I have taken it upon myself to write. I believe your daughter to be in need of her family, but we cannot risk sending her to you. I shall leave it to you to determine which of her family would be of greatest benefit. If you will consent to a visit, please send your reply, and we shall assist with all the arrangements.

Your Servant,
Matthias Addison

Consequences

September 20, 1813
Pemberley, Derbyshire

Dear Richard,

Allow me to wish you joy on your betrothal to Lady Amelia. She suits you well, and I have every expectation of your future happiness. Though after seeing the two of you together, I know not how you will survive a four-month engagement. Your plan to remove to Finmere Park is a sound one, I think. Certainly your staff will need time to prepare for a new mistress and, as I recall, there was some work yet to be done on the master's and mistress's chambers.

I would advise you not to make any changes to the mistress's suite without first consulting your betrothed. My time with both Georgiana and the Bennet sisters has taught me nothing if not that knowledge of the preferences and tastes of a lady is no excuse to arrange things on her behalf without first seeking her opinion. To do so is, according to the ladies, "officious, presumptuous, and rude," regardless of how well intended the action may be. Please do not seek further explanation as I fear I cannot give it.

Georgiana and I were pleased to learn that Lady Hargrove is safely delivered of a daughter. Hargrove seems not disappointed in the least in not having an heir and, instead, appears to rejoice in a daughter who strongly favours her mother. Your father, naturally, had much to say on the point but was kind enough to limit his audience to myself. A wise decision on his part, for I do not think Hargrove cares to hear any strictures against his wife or child. For my part, I am in agreement with Hargrove. To have both mother and child safe and well must be cause for celebration.

I shall pause here as Georgiana has come to remind me of a promised afternoon ride.

September 21

If ever I have the grave misfortune of encountering that snivelling, pathetic weasel, I shall kill him with my bare hands. But, of course, you do not know of whom I speak. I shall tell you—it is that insolent, reprehensible parson of my aunt's.

I received an express from Addison last night. As you know, Aunt Catherine has been in town for some weeks and only just returned to Kent. Matthias and Anne had been some three days returned from their wedding trip when our cousin became concerned at the absence of Miss Elizabeth. Prior to the wedding, it had been her

custom to call on Rosings every day. When Miss Elizabeth had not visited after three days, our aunt and cousin
determined to call on the lady to discern the reason. Mr
Collins had barred all visitors, but the servants of that
house are loyal to their mistress and to our aunt, thus
Lady Catherine and Anne were admitted at once. What
they found at the parsonage was too horrific to bear
repeating. Miss Elizabeth refused to speak against Mr
Collins, but I am given to understand the servants had no
such qualms. Upon confirming the source of Miss
Elizabeth's injuries, my aunt summoned the local
apothecary to administer laudanum to Miss Elizabeth
and then immediately arranged for her removal to
Rosings Park. There she has remained these many days.

Addison has notified her family in Hertfordshire, and I
can only hope Mr Bennet has the good sense to travel
with one or two of his daughters and to leave his wife at
home. I would wish the woman to see and perhaps finally
feel the true effect of her decision, but I fear her presence
would only distress my precious Elizabeth at a time when
she most needs peace. Miss Elizabeth has been offered
permanent sanctuary at Rosings. It is the belief of my
aunt, and I cannot disagree, that Mr Collins's sycophantic
tendencies towards herself will prevent his acting to
reclaim his wife. Would that such actions had been taken
months ago!

I have written to Addison to suggest a guard for his new
guest and offered to bear the cost. I am certain that, as
Miss Elizabeth begins to recover, she will at some time or
other wish to wander the lanes and paths of Rosings. This
cannot but end in disaster for her. I shudder to think what

that hateful man would do should he chance to have the opportunity.

I wish to travel to Rosings immediately, but I know I cannot. What possible excuse could I give for such a visit and how would I stay my hand and not disgrace my family? I am in need of your counsel—or perhaps just your sword.

Yours, etc.
Fitzwilliam Darcy

❧

September 21, 1813
Rosings Park, Kent

Dear Mr Bennet,

It is with gratitude and relief we have received your reply. We shall expect you and your daughters on the morrow.

Matthias Addison

❧

October 1813, Longbourn

"Oh, Mr Bennet, you are too cruel! You cannot force me to leave my home!" Mrs Bennet cried. "I only did what was necessary to secure my future and that of our girls. We would have been cast into the hedgerows if you had not lived!"

Mr Bennet would not be moved. "You will find, Mrs Bennet,

that I can do that and worse. Your actions, against my clearly expressed wishes I might add, nearly resulted in the death of my daughter. I have ordered repairs on the dowager cottage to be completed immediately. Until then, you are not to leave your rooms. If I find you have defied me in this, you will find yourself cut off from every possible manner of support and protection afforded you as mistress of this estate."

Mrs Bennet turned wild eyes to the others in the room, coming to rest first on Mary who said solemnly, "whatsoever a man soweth, that shall he also reap." She then returned her attention to her father, hoping he would stand firm.

Mrs Bennet looked next to her youngest daughters for support. "Lydia, child, surely you do not wish to be separated from your mama? Catherine, who will teach you to catch a fine husband?"

While Catherine could only look at her mother and walk away, Lydia replied, "I do not particularly like your way of getting husbands," and joined her sister above stairs.

October 15, 1813
Netherfield Park, Hertfordshire

Dear Richard,

I am pleased to know everything is progressing as planned at Finmere. Until you wrote of it, I had not considered how difficult it might be for two people to agree upon so simple a thing as wall fabrics and paints. It should, I suppose, be expected that a military man and a woman of fashion might have disparate tastes. Having heard your story, I can only advise that you yield to the preference of your betrothed in these things except, perhaps, as it pertains to your study. In that space, I can see no reason why your choices should not prevail. I look forward to viewing the completed rooms and can only hope to be as conservative with your brandy as you have always been with mine.

Though I have not yet conquered the desire to harm that miserable toad in Kent, I have taken your advice and travelled to Hertfordshire. We plan to remain here until we travel to Ashford for the Christmas season. Georgiana was especially pleased as this has afforded her the opportunity to renew her friendship with the Bennet sisters. I must confess I am no less pleased to be here. To be in the company of Elizabeth's family is an unexpected joy. Two years ago, I could not have been prevailed upon to make such a statement and would have dismissed any suggestion of association. Now I find myself quite content to be amongst them and to share in their daily trials and triumphs. I anticipate Miss Bennet's radiant smile after having a successful debate with her father, Miss Catherine's pleasure when the afternoon light is precisely as she wished for her newest sketch, and Miss Lydia's glee at mastering a new piece of music. I have learnt Mr Bennet was an accomplished student of debate during his time at Oxford. He has proven to be an excellent conversationalist and a worthy chess adversary. I daresay even your father would be hard-pressed to defeat this gentleman in either debate or a game. How very much poorer I should have been without these delightful ladies and their estimable father.

Of their mother, I cannot say too little.

Bingley has settled upon an estate, and he will make the

purchase by month's end. He does not intend to take possession until spring as another little Bingley is scheduled to arrive in January. Grey Manor is but ten miles from Pemberley, and as Miss Catherine will live with her eldest sister after the move, I expect we shall exchange frequent visits. Georgiana is in raptures at the promise of having a friend situated so near to her. Miss Bennet and Miss Lydia will likely often be guests at one or other of the homes. Miss Lydia has lately begun applying to her father for the purchase of a harp and was most happy to learn she might practice on the one at Pemberley whenever she should visit.

Mr Bennet, Miss Bennet, and Mrs Bingley are lately returned from Kent. Mrs Bingley is inclined to speak only in the best terms of her sister's continued improvement, but one can see the tightening around her eyes and a slight pursing of her lips when she does so. Mr Bennet and Miss Bennet are more forward with their concerns, but not in the presence of Miss Catherine or Miss Lydia. From the three travellers I am given to understand that, while Elizabeth's physical injuries are healing well, her spirit suffers greatly. I do not believe I have ever seen Mr Bennet so moved to action. That he was unhappy regarding Elizabeth's marriage is no great secret; however, I believe encountering the unpleasant truth of her situation in such a direct manner has reawakened his outrage as nothing else might have done. He has begun repairs on the former dowager house at Longbourn, and he says Mrs Bennet will be removed to that location as soon as it is liveable.

Mrs Bennet faces other consequences as well. She is no longer included in any invitation to her daughter's home, the younger Miss Bennets spend the better part of each day away from her presence, and though the specific circumstances are not generally known, the fact that she is so often excluded from her family party has been much remarked upon and resulted in a narrowing of her social circle. In short, the lady who forced this situation now finds herself very much alone. I save my compassion for her daughter.

Your cousin,
Fitzwilliam Darcy

🙰

November 1, 1813
Rosings Park, Kent

Dear Jane,

Grey Manor sounds perfectly charming, and I think you and my brother are quite wise to take possession in the spring. To undertake a move in the winter, and so close to your confinement would be arduous indeed. I am sorry to hear Mama has been so trying; perhaps it will make the time of removal less burdensome as you will be relieved to be out of her daily presence. To take Catherine with you is a kindness I am certain she will appreciate.

I should thank you and Mary again and again for your kind attentions in September. I am sure if Papa had come alone he would have been quite at a loss, and I confess that I was in great need of your company as well. My hostess tells me I should inform my family of my continued recovery, though I have been loath to write of it as I do not believe words can adequately express how greatly changed I am from the poor bedraggled creature of September. I shall start with the area of least recovery. I am certain you will not be surprised to learn that I do not sleep well at all. Indeed my cousin plagues my dreams so that I have little desire to engage in the activity.

Not all my news is so terrible. My appetite for both food and life is returning, and I must say that Rosings is an excellent place to recover one's spirits, though not perhaps so excellent as Pemberley proved to be last spring. Lady Catherine and Anne have been most attentive in making sure every meal contains some or other favourite of mine. They were quite convinced, as I believe you were, that I was too thin before. I have very nearly recovered my former energy and can now enjoy frequent walks about the grounds. I had not realised how greatly I missed my morning rambles. Fret not, for I am never without an escort. I do try not to chaff at this restriction, as I understand the necessity of such measures. The escort is not nearly so much an insult to my desire for independence as being restricted to the parsonage had been for so many months.

I thank you and my brother for the kind invitation to join you first at Netherfield and then on to Grey Manor. As much as I would wish to be able to accept, I fear it is impossible. So long as Mr Collins retains a legal claim on my life, I am best beyond his reach here. I shall not scruple to say I would not likely come to Netherfield in any case. Mama has been vigorous in her objections to my current status, and I cannot conceive of placing you or any of the rest of my family in what would surely be a most awkward position. Perhaps if Papa carries through with his plans to remove her to the dowager house, I might reconsider. Until then I am quite resigned to live out my days at Rosings in this strange state of being neither single nor truly married.

November 4, 1813

Oh, Jane surely you will think me to be the most unnatural creature that ever was when you read these next lines. I had just set my mind to close this letter when an unexpected visitor arrived. You can well imagine how guarded the entire household has been of late, so I do not exaggerate when I say the man was nearly turned away before he could state what he was about. He was an assistant to the local magistrate. It seems a carriage was found overturned on the London road that very morning. The driver and passenger both suffered mortal injuries.

To be very plain, sister, I am now a widow. Mr Collins is dead. I confess to you alone that I felt nothing but relief at the news. There, I have said it, and you may judge me as uncaring and unnatural as may be.

It has now been three days since we heard the report of my cousin's demise. As I am his nearest relative (in fact our family are his only living relations) it fell to me to make the arrangements. I shall not deceive you: I was most pleased to leave the entire matter to Mr Addison. I hardly know what more to write save that I am grateful that the support of my dear friends means I do not have to determine the course of my future today.

Your unashamedly relieved sister,
Elizabeth Collins (might I ever rid myself of his name?)

FREE

November 6, 1813
Darcy House, London

Dear Richard,

Georgiana and I departed Hertfordshire somewhat sooner than anticipated. If you are still of a mind to receive visitors, we shall be happy to join you at Finmere for some weeks. May G-d forgive me, I can find naught but joy in the cause of our removal. Bingley and Mr Bennet have gone to Kent in response to news from that quarter.

Mrs Bingley received an express from Elizabeth two days past. Mr Collins is dead, and my Elizabeth is a widow. I have been assured she does not regret the loss. Elizabeth's letter said only there had been a carriage accident.

Being possessed of a naturally inquisitive nature, I sent my own express to Addison in hopes of learning further details. I was immensely satisfied with his prompt reply.

It appears Mr Collins was not so subject to the will of our
aunt as had first been supposed and had begun to investi-
gate how he might remove Elizabeth from our aunt's care.
He did not think to find sympathy or assistance in Kent
and therefore determined to travel to London. In his haste
to depart, he gave no consideration to the conditions of
the road or the time of day; instead, he waved his purse
about the local inn until some desperate soul agreed to
begin the journey though dark was rapidly approaching
and a recent storm had left the roads in remarkably poor
condition. Apparently, it is true that money does not buy
sense. The next morning the carriage was found
overturned and both the driver and Mr Collins had
sustained mortal injuries. Though it was not disclosed to
Elizabeth, the magistrate believes Mr Collins did not
perish instantly but rather suffered from his wounds for
some time. You may think me unnatural and cruel, but I
can only hope the magistrate is correct in his beliefs. Not
even with Wickham have I ever before wished such a fate
on my fellow man.

Mr and Mrs Addison have offered a home to Elizabeth for
as long as she wishes to remain in their care. They have
extended that hospitality to whichever of her sisters she
wishes to invite. It is odd to think of Elizabeth in
permanent residence at Rosings. I could not have imagined such a thing coming to pass. I do not know what this
change in Elizabeth's status will mean for me. Perhaps
nothing. It is not likely I shall see the lady until we visit
Kent in March, and even then, she will not yet be in half-
mourning.

I do hope to at least renew our acquaintance at that time
and determine whether there is even a possibility I might

someday earn her approbation. What a terrible fate that would be—to at last be free to pursue Elizabeth only to discover she does not care for me. It is not a thought I care to dwell upon. Instead, I shall rejoice that she is at last safe and free.

Your unabashedly grateful cousin,
Fitzwilliam Darcy

December 15, 1813
Rosings Park, Kent

Dear Jane,

It is nearly impossible to think that another Christmas is nearly upon us. I had thought to come to you at Nether-field to join in the family celebrations. However, I find that is no longer possible. I have in my possession a letter from Mama making it very clear that, despite the entail having been broken with my cousin's death, I am still very much out of favour with that lady. She blames me for Mr Collins's death and says I failed in my duty by not producing an heir. There is more, but in the end, she says I am no longer welcome at Longbourn. I fear the breach between us is now complete.

Though I know my father would easily overrule his wife, I have no wish to subject myself to Mama's temper, and no matter how I miss all my family, I cannot add to the disruption of the household. Therefore, I shall have to wait some time before seeing you all again. Do not worry for me; I shall not spend the holiday alone. Anne's Aunt

Fitzwilliam, Lady Matlock, has graciously included me in the general invitation to spend the holiday season with the Fitzwilliam-Darcy-De Bourgh families at Ashford Lodge. Mr and Mrs Addison will travel to Bath to be with his family while I go with Lady Catherine to Derbyshire. I am given to understand it is a lovely estate, and I confess that the thought of spending the season with a large family, even if it is not my own, gives me pleasure.

I have enclosed some small gifts for my family, even my mother. I dare not send them directly to Longbourn so I shall trust you to have them safely delivered.

Happy Christmas, dear sister.
Elizabeth

December 1813, Ashford Lodge, Derbyshire

THE COMBINED Fitzwilliam and Darcy families were gathered in a large sitting room speaking of Christmases long past and laughing together over their shared childhood exploits. Elizabeth joined in where she could and shared a few tales of her own.

Mr Darcy used the opportunity to ask the lady at his side. "How do you find Ashford?"

"I think it second only to Pemberley in beauty. Pray do not tell your aunt I said so. I would not wish to appear ungrateful," Elizabeth replied with a slight smile.

"I do not think you are capable of such a thing. Perhaps later in the week, Georgiana and I might introduce you to the sculpture garden. It is situated near enough to the house as to be easily accessible even in winter, and the path is well maintained."

"I should like that very much, Mr Darcy. Anne speaks well of her time at Ashford Lodge, and I find I wish to experience it myself."

Georgiana spoke then, "Oh, brother, we must take Elizabeth for a sleigh ride!"

Lady Matlock heard this and gave her support to the scheme. "You should make a party of it. We have sleighs and horses enough to spare. Only tell me when you wish to go out, and I shall have refreshments waiting for your return."

The idea gained universal approval, and the following evening, three sleighs were readied for the outing. Lady Amelia joined Richard, the Viscount and his wife took the second sleigh, and Elizabeth and Georgiana were bundled into the third with Darcy. The horses moved at a steady pace over the grounds, and Elizabeth's eyes were filled with wonder. Snow clung to hedges and trees like a soft blanket while icicles hung glistening in the faint light of the moon. Georgiana clutched Elizabeth's right hand in her left and laughed as the snow began to fall. Across from them, Darcy wondered whether he had ever seen anyone as lovely as the woman across from him with her eyes alight with joy and a smile dancing across her face.

December 27, 1813
Ashford Lodge, Derbyshire

Dear Bingley,

I write solely to bring your family news of their beloved sister. Georgiana and I arrived at Ashford Lodge with Richard on December 10. We were joined over the next several days by the Viscount and Countess Hargrove and Lady Amelia. The most welcome addition to our family party joined us on the seventeenth when Elizabeth arrived in the company of Lady Catherine. I do not have to tell you: I had no need of further gifts.

Elizabeth is so greatly changed from when I last saw her as to astonish me. She is very nearly restored to her former self. Though I have not yet heard her laugh, I have seen her smile every day. We are quite often thrown together as, with the exception of Lady Catherine, the rest of the party are paired off in couples. Georgiana is quite taken with Elizabeth, and the two of them often entertain the company with a duet. When Elizabeth is not reading or playing, she is most likely to be found walking through the sculpture gardens, which are especially enchanting this time of year. I take great delight in joining her as often as possible, and I am sometimes accompanied by Georgiana. She was particularly delighted when she joined Georgiana and me for a sleigh ride about the park. The ladies were well protected with thick blankets and warming stones for their hands and feet. Once we began the tour, a smile that was, I am certain, entirely too wide to be strictly proper spread across her face, and there it remained for several hours. We returned rosy-cheeked and quite ready for the hot chocolate my aunt had requested.

I do not think I exaggerate when I say this holiday has been most agreeable for Elizabeth. She has been well received by all my family. Indeed, it is as if she has always been among us. Your sister has a remarkable talent for setting everyone at ease with her manners and speech. She has regaled the company with tales of Christmas among four sisters and takes delight in every story told in return. Though there is a light in your sister's eyes that I had thought long extinguished, there is also a hint of sadness there when she speaks of her family; I believe she misses them dearly.

Georgiana has informed me of a desire to invite Miss Bennet, Miss Catherine, and Miss Lydia to Pemberley in the spring, and though Georgiana has not yet said so, I am certain the invitation will be extended to include Elizabeth. I must ask you to keep this information in confidence as we would not like any of the ladies to be disappointed if there is a change in our plans. Perhaps when she is again in the company of her sisters, I shall be privileged to hear Elizabeth laugh.

Yours in friendship,
Fitzwilliam Darcy

January 31, 1814
Ashford Lodge, Derbyshire

Dear Jane,

Once again, I offer my congratulations on the arrival of my niece. Despite the testimony of her grandfather, I believe it is much too early to say she has my disposition. Surely, with two such agreeable parents, any daughter of yours must be infinitely more complying than her aunt could ever hope to be. I am happy to learn you passed the holidays in relative peace and that our dear Catherine has decided to follow you to Derbyshire.

We leave tomorrow to return to Rosings. Our holiday in Ashford has been all that is delightful. Georgiana asks that I pass on her regards to Mary, Catherine, and Lydia. I believe she intends to invite them to visit her at Pemberley—only do not say anything as I would not wish to disappoint our sisters if the event should be postponed. As Catherine is going with you and I hope to have Mary join me, perhaps she will have to settle for Lydia alone. It seems that would be of benefit to both as Lydia's liveliness might lessen Georgiana's reserve and from Georgiana, Lydia might learn some little restraint. With Catherine and Mary both absent from Longbourn, I fear a little for Lydia as she will have no elder sisters to guide her and may turn again to her mother for companionship. Perhaps we might take turns to host her. Both Anne and Lady Catherine have expressed again and again that I may invite any of my family to come whenever I am so inclined.

As you have guessed, we were joined at Ashford Lodge by Georgiana and Mr Darcy. Also in the family party were Colonel Fitzwilliam and his elder brother and his wife, Viscount and Countess Hargrove. It was quite a large gathering, and everyone seemed determined to display as much affection and love as could be had. Having spent no small amount of time with Lady Catherine and Mr Darcy, I confess I was surprised at the open warmth of the family, though I suppose I should not be. After all, Aunt and Uncle Gardiner are not at all similar to our own parents.

Mr Darcy amongst his family is a revelation. Gone is his taciturn disposition and reserve, replaced by a gentleman who is all ease and friendliness. He seemed somehow lighter in his bearing than ever he was last summer. It was as if a great weight had been lifted from his shoulders. I found myself frequently in company with Mr Darcy and Georgiana as everyone else was naturally paired off. In Colonel Fitzwilliam's case, his frequent partner was his betrothed, Lady Amelia, who is the daughter of an earl. I understand the colonel has done his duty to both his family and himself by having the good sense to fall in love with an heiress. We had sleigh rides about the grounds, and there was even a snowball fight or two. Mr Darcy and Colonel Fitzwilliam were utterly incorrigible. Lady Matlock only shook her head at them and muttered something that sounded distinctly like, "Boys. They never do grow up!" I had to smile at the picture of Mr Darcy and the colonel as boys.

I spent much of my time agreeably engaged reading, playing duets with Georgiana, or walking about the gardens near the house. My escort at Ashford Lodge was far more pleasant than the ones with which I am familiar from Rosings. Will you think badly of me when I say that Mr Darcy often found reason to walk with me and that I made no move to discourage him? We were sometimes joined by Georgiana, but just as often, it was only we two. I daresay we are now great friends.

As I hinted earlier, and only after much discussion, Anne has persuaded me to invite Mary to Rosings for a time. I believe our sister would do well away from the censure of my mother and having a companion would be quite agreeable to me, as it would enable me to accept invitations to travel without inconveniencing my hostess. That said companion could also be a dear sister is only a source of additional joy.

Your inexplicably happy sister,
Elizabeth

P.S. You see I have divested myself of his name at least in writing.

January 31, 1814
Ashford Lodge, Derbyshire

Dear Mary,

I am exceedingly pleased to know you have decided to accept my invitation. I believe you will find Rosings very much to your liking. There is an extensive library and the most beautiful pianoforte to practice your music. As Lady Catherine delights in listening to others perform, perhaps we may learn a few duets to play for the family.

Anne asks me to inform you she and Mr Addison will travel to London next week for Colonel Fitzwilliam's marriage to Lady Amelia on February 9. The Addisons will return to Rosings the following day and are most willing for you to join them if Papa would bring you first to Darcy House in town.

I am anxiously awaiting your arrival.

Your truly delighted sister,
Elizabeth

January 31, 1814
Ashford Lodge, Derbyshire

Dear Bingley,

I have learnt from Elizabeth that you are to be congratulated on the birth of your daughter. I must tell you—as I
know she will not—the aunt was quite overcome to know
her niece would bear her name. I am also informed that
Mr Bennet has already ascribed his favourite daughter's
personality to young Hannah Elizabeth. If he is correct, I
can only say you and Mrs Bingley will benefit from the
liveliness of such a child.

Tomorrow we shall depart Ashford Lodge for London
where we plan to remain until after Richard's wedding. I
fear I must arrive early if for no reason other than to
protect my brandy. The man has utterly charmed my staff
and has no compunction in helping himself to my stores.
Georgiana has dispatched an invitation to Miss Lydia to
join us in London before travelling with us to Pemberley.
As you will recall, she had first planned to invite all the
sisters, but we are given to understand Elizabeth has
invited Miss Bennet to join her at Rosings, and Miss
Catherine is determined to assist Mrs Bingley with the
children.

I rather suspect my pocketbook will be considerably
lighter before the visit is complete. Georgiana has spoken
rather often of the need to gift her friend with music,
ribbons, lace, and I know not what else. I only know there
are excursions planned to Bond Street. I attempt to look
stern and put-upon whenever the topic is broached; it

will not do for my sister to know how pleased I am to indulge both her and Miss Lydia in this manner.

I was pleased with your intelligence as regards Mrs Bennet. I had wondered whether Mr Bennet would hold to his resolution, and it seems he has. As you are no doubt already aware, Mr Collins was the last male relative of Mr Bennet, and the entail was broken upon that man's death. As none of Longbourn's lands are held by the crown, Mr Bennet is free to do as he will with the estate. I have referred him to my solicitor in London for advice on the matter. The comfort of knowing the estate will not pass to some unknown relative has certainly increased his interest in Longbourn's management, and I believe better management to be responsible for the funds required to repair the dower house and provide some few servants for its maintenance. Of course, a reduction in Mrs Bennet's pin money was also helpful. I cannot but agree with Mr Bennet's reasoning. A woman who finds herself with a very small social circle and who no longer entertains, surely has not so many needs as she might have previously. Knowing she cannot be happy with her new situation, I have great compassion for the servants attending Mrs Bennet. For their sake, I hope they are well compensated.

Your decision to take possession of Grey Manor in April is an excellent scheme. You, Mrs Bingley, and Miss Catherine are welcome to stay at Pemberley while any work is being completed. At such an easy distance, it will be nothing for you to travel between the two estates. I shall likely join you in the effort. With so many ladies present, we cannot think they will always be in need of our company. It is unfortunate Mr Bennet does not care to travel; else, he could join us as well. In truth, I suspect it is more a wish for some small measure of solitude than a real disgust of travel that motivates his decision to remain in Hertfordshire at this time. If you decide to come to Pemberley, you need only write. I would have no opposition to an unplanned visit, but Mrs Reynolds is likely to prefer time to prepare your rooms, and as I wish to remain in that lady's good graces, I beg your indulgence in this.

Until then, I remain...
Your friend,
Fitzwilliam Darcy

February 15, 1814
Darcy House, London

Dear Anne,

Well Cousin, I must first say how delighted both Georgiana and I were with your news. I am certain you and Matthias will be excellent parents. I am not in the least surprised that your mother has already planned the nursery and am only astonished she has not decreed when the child should arrive. Truly, 'tis a mark of her enthusiasm to become a grandmother, I think. Richard tells me the quest for grandchildren is all he has heard from his mother since the day he announced his betrothal, and now that he is wed, he has no expectation of change in that quarter.

It was very kind of you to convey Miss Bennet to her

sister. I believe you will find the young woman to be a welcome addition to your household. She is a sensible sort of girl who is well-read and plays beautifully. I think she will flourish in her new environment, and I know she has truly missed her sister. Though your mother may not have been so kind to her before making Elizabeth's acquaintance, I believe even she will think Mary worthy, and I have long thought Elizabeth would benefit from being more with her family.

I have reason to hope you will not have much time to become acquainted with Miss Bennet until, perhaps, this summer. The enclosed letter from Georgiana invites the pair to Pemberley for a lengthy visit. I had urged her to wait and extend the invitation closer to summer, but she will not be gainsaid in this. I suspect her insistence is born as much from Miss Lydia's desire to see her elder sister as it is from Georgiana's wish to further her friendship with both ladies. Miss Lydia was somewhat put out regarding our imminent departure until she learnt of the possibility of seeing Elizabeth. It would appear that, while five days of visiting the shops are not sufficient to satisfy all her desires, being again in the presence of a sister she once thought lost to her is a greater temptation. Since learning of Georgiana's plan to invite Elizabeth and Miss Bennet to Pemberley, Miss Lydia has spoken of nothing else. I am bid to ask you not to reveal Miss Lydia's presence as I am told it is to be a great surprise for Elizabeth when she arrives. My exposure to the Bennet sisters has left me in no doubt of the ability of the female mind to plan and execute a course of action. I have come to think our generals might be better off allowing their wives to plan their campaigns. Surely, there is none so formidable as a determined woman, as I am certain you very well know.

As we hope to have more visitors, we are not planning to join you for Easter this year. Perhaps Richard and Lady Amelia's presence will atone for our absence. If the weather holds, we shall depart for Pemberley tomorrow. Miss Lydia has never before stayed at an inn, nor has she travelled so great a distance. It will be refreshing to view the journey through new eyes.

Your cousin,
Fitzwilliam Darcy

COMING HOME

March 1814, Pemberley

ELIZABETH'S second visit to Pemberley was no less anticipated than her first and her greeting on arrival even more enthusiastic. She had scarcely stepped from the carriage before being engulfed in the arms of her youngest sister.

"Lizzy!" Lydia shouted as she ran, and Elizabeth was so overcome with happiness that she could not reprimand her lively sister's lack of decorum. This was her Lydia—wild, fierce, and independent as always. Mary thought to admonish their sister but could not. Instead, she walked to Elizabeth's side and wrapped her arms around both sisters. In Elizabeth's heart, she began to feel as though she had finally come home.

The following days were spent in idle pleasure. Nature was kind enough to grace them with several days of sunshine, of which Elizabeth took full advantage. She spent each morning on a different path. Her favourite meandered around the pond, over a small bridge to the woods, then back to the house. Mr Darcy found her there the first morning. "Good morning," he greeted her.

"And a good morning to you as well, sir. I hope I am not intruding."

"Not at all. If anything, it would seem I have interrupted your privacy on your morning stroll."

Elizabeth smiled at that. "Nonsense, Mr Darcy. You are the master of this house and may come and go as you please. I am only a guest."

"Be that as it may, you were here first. Therefore, I shall ask, may I join you?"

"I would be honoured, sir," Elizabeth replied and allowed him to place her hand on his arm. They walked in companionable silence for some time before Darcy took his leave and returned to the house.

Elizabeth thought it mere coincidence when he found her again the next day. This time she was in the formal rose gardens. "This garden was a favourite of my mother," he said by way of greeting.

"I can easily see why," Elizabeth commented as he fell in step beside her and once again they walked together for a time, speaking of inconsequential matters before returning to the house.

This continued each day. Elizabeth would choose a path in the morning, and no matter where her feet took her, Mr Darcy was sure to follow. He came with offerings of fruit and bread and even a thin volume of poetry, which he said his mother once preferred to read under a particular tree near their chosen path.

To both their consternation, after the third day, they were joined by Mary each time they walked together. How she managed to locate them remained a mystery.

March 5, 1814
Pemberley, Derbyshire

Dear Jane,

As you see from the direction on my letter, Mary and I have travelled to Pemberley to visit Georgiana and Lydia. We hope to also see Catherine and your family whilst we are here. I had not the least intention of coming so soon, but Georgiana can be most persuasive, and I found I could not decline so well phrased an invitation as hers. There was, of course, the added inducement of being once again in the company of my sisters. I believe the timing of the visits was rather carefully planned for it seems too great a coincidence that we should all chance to be at Pemberley at the same time. Each time I am reunited with one of my sisters, I think I can feel no greater joy than I do in those first moments of restoration.

Our sisters are so greatly changed! Lydia is still herself— fiercely independent and livelier than what is entirely acceptable, and yet she is wholly proper. Mary is still quiet, bookish, and reserved, but she has discovered the works of Donne and Wordsworth and has developed a love of history, much to my relief. Lydia has abandoned the pianoforte, but she is becoming quite proficient on Georgiana's harp, and Mary's playing is now simply delightful. They are so improved that we are now able to have an entire conversation without a single mention of officers, fashion, or the great Reverend Fordyce. To be honest, the improvement in them makes me feel a little ashamed that I did not make a greater effort towards them much sooner.

Mr Darcy had thought to go to London for a time, but finding no support for this scheme, he soon abandoned it.

Georgiana and Lydia are not yet out (Lydia herself declared this much to my astonishment), Mary is not at all inclined to visit town, and I am supposed to still be in mourning though I have scandalised our sister by refusing to wear black. I daresay if she had been married to that man, she would not mourn him either, and I care not one jot for society's opinion on the subject except as how it might bring harm to my sisters. We are all content to remain at Pemberley, for who could not approve of such a magical place?

We shall likely remain in Derbyshire at least until summer, enjoying all the estate has to offer. I have already discovered several pathways on which to lose myself. Mr Darcy always manages to find me—a circumstance that never fails to brighten my day. Here at Pemberley I feel entirely free; even the spectre of our cousin does not appear in my dreams.

Your unfashionably impertinent sister,
Elizabeth

March 10, 1814
Pemberley, Derbyshire

Dear Bingley,

Where previously I mentioned a stay at Pemberley purely out of courtesy, I now write to beg your presence and that of Mrs Bingley and Miss Catherine. Elizabeth and Miss Bennet have been here some three weeks, and I cannot tell you the pleasure reflected in Elizabeth's eyes when she beheld her youngest sister. I can only think that the presence of all her sisters would bring her even greater joy. I shall be happy to provide whatever assistance is necessary to facilitate your early journey hence.

Yours in friendship,
Fitzwilliam Darcy

༄

March 10, 1814
Pemberley, Derbyshire

Dear Richard,

I am glad to know Lady Amelia is pleased with the work completed at Finmere and that the pair of you are well settled. I have taken the liberty of adding to your cellar a case of my finest brandy. I harbour no expectation of it remaining long in the bottle, but I do hope you at least raise your glass to me when you drink it. Tilson tells me your steward is performing admirably. He even went so far as to say he had some hope of your successful transition from soldier to landowner. Coming from him, this is high praise indeed. I do not believe I have ever heard him speak so highly of another. The last time he even hinted at speaking well of someone, he only said the man was nearly as useful as his favourite horse. I have also looked over the investments you are considering, and I am so much in favour of your plans as to say I shall likely make some of my own. I believe the future will belong to those who are wise enough to expand their interests beyond the land.

Hargrove has written to inform me he is in search of a

small estate to purchase. It is his intention to settle the place on a second son should he be so fortunate as to have one. If not, he will settle it on a daughter as part of her dowry. I do admire the man's forethought. Should I ever be so fortunate as to marry and have children of my own, I shall follow his example in providing for my daughters and younger sons.

Have I thanked you for forcing me to return to Hertfordshire two years ago? If not, allow me to do so now. Elizabeth and her sisters have been here for almost three weeks, and each day is better than the last. If I could spend the remainder of my days at Pemberley with Elizabeth, I should die a happy man—giggling sisters and chaos notwithstanding. Elizabeth has the endearing habit of attempting to lose herself on some lane or other nearly every day. I have made a game of attempting to discover her whereabouts and join her on her rambles.

I am rather impressed at her refusal to wear black during her supposed mourning. It takes tremendous courage to defy expectations in this manner. Miss Bennet, I think, was rather scandalised at her sister's choice, but I find I cannot fault Elizabeth's reasoning. She is in a place where she is not known and has no reason to fear censure either for herself or for her sisters. Given her temperament and the nature of her marriage, I think it would be against her character to pretend feelings she could never possess.

Even though she is not yet out of mourning, her own opinion on the matter has left me feeling rather free to begin a sort of courtship, and I have endeavoured to act accordingly whenever I am in her company. I can only hope she does not find me too forward. As she is not a lady impressed by standing or wealth, I find I must be more creative in my gifts to her. To that end, I have written Bingley to beg the presence of his family as soon as possible.

I am of the opinion that Elizabeth will be as pleased with the presence of all her sisters as most ladies would be in receiving the crown jewels. I had hoped to entice Mr Bennet into joining us; however, he has expressed a reluctance to travel such a distance. For my part, I believe he is not convinced Mrs Bennet will abide by his restrictions in his absence, and he has no interest in being further embarrassed by the actions of his wife. Additionally, Bingley informs me that Mr Bennet is suffering no small amount of guilt over Elizabeth's situation, and he has not yet determined how he will face her. Convincing Mr Bennet of his absolution is no small task. I know my Elizabeth bears her father no ill will and, in fact, places the responsibility for her marriage and subsequent unhappiness entirely on her mother and husband. Elizabeth well understands her father had once forbidden the match with Collins and was in no state to object when her mother brought the thing about.

The subject of Mrs Bennet is the only one that no one dares broach. It causes Elizabeth a good deal of pain, and none here are willing to subject her to such a thing. When we speak of her family, we speak only of her father and sisters. I know she longs to see her father again, and I am determined to see that happen.

I had thought to escort the ladies to town to partake of some amusement there, but the scheme was not as charming as I had imagined, and it was soundly rejected.

Miss Lydia informed me that, as she and Georgiana are not out, there is very little to engage them. Miss Bennet does not yet feel equal to appearing in society, and Elizabeth said not even she would be so bold as to be seen in town during the season when she is supposed to be in mourning. I do not regret the outcome; as you know, I am always happy to remain at Pemberley. I confess to being far more entertained here than I had imagined at first. The ladies provide excellent music and conversation, and I find it is rarely dull when they are about.

I would suggest you and Lady Amelia join us when you grow weary of one another's company, but as I think that to be an unlikely event, I shall only suggest you come to us on your way to Kent. Bingley should have arrived by then, and I have no doubt Lady Amelia will be delighted to make the acquaintance of Mrs Bingley and her children. Even if that were not the case, I know I shall be in need of male reinforcements after being outnumbered in my own house for such a long period of time.

Until then, I remain
Your cousin,
Fitzwilliam Darcy

April 1814, Pemberley

"Lizzy! Come quickly! Mr Darcy has a surprise for you!" Lydia called through the library to her elder sister.

"Lydia, there is no need to yell," Mary admonished.

"You will not discourage me today, Mary, for you know as well as I what he has done!"

"It seems I *should* be concerned if Mr Darcy is conspiring with my sisters," Elizabeth said to stop the impending argument.

"Pish! You know very well he would sooner give up his estate than harm you!" Lydia replied.

Elizabeth blushed at her suggestion. "In any case, we should not keep him waiting," she said and laid her book aside to follow her sisters.

On reaching the front hall, Elizabeth was overcome with joy on seeing not only Catherine and Jane, but also Jane's children. Darcy stood quietly to one side with Bingley, observing the reunion with no small degree of pleasure.

Having been once again reunited with a missed and beloved sister, Elizabeth spoke to Darcy that evening, "If I did not know better, sir, I would think you are courting me."

"Who says I am not?"

April 10, 1814
Pemberley, Derbyshire

Dear Uncle,

I find myself in need of your advice. You will, I am certain, recall making the acquaintance of Mrs Elizabeth Collins last Christmas, and of course, you are aware of the lady's history as you have been a source of guidance for me in the past where she is concerned.

Miss Elizabeth has been a guest of Georgiana these past two months, and I find myself as much in her power as I ever was. She is almost wholly restored to the woman I first met so long ago in Hertfordshire. She is intelligent and determined with a marvellous sense of humour. She challenges me as often as she delights me, and I find myself wishing to make her an offer. Until I began to contemplate a proposal, I had not questioned my reception.

But now I am beset with doubts. How do I ask her to throw aside convention and marry me? How can I know she will accept an offer after having such an abysmal experience in her first marriage? If we marry before her mourning is ended, will I materially damage the chances of not only my sister, but hers as well, to make a good match? Will I destroy any hope of her being accepted in our circle? These and a thousand other questions plague my waking moments. I find all my confidence has deserted me in the face of these fears. I would by no means wish to destroy her happiness. Tell me, uncle, what am I to do?

Your nephew,
Fitzwilliam Darcy

Incandescently Happy

May 1814, Pemberley

ELIZABETH SAT LEANING against the window and watching as raindrops gathered on the glass before streaming in rivulets down the pane. Her plans to walk near the pond had been quickly set aside when she woke to the sound of thunder in the pre-dawn hours. Resolved to enjoy her day regardless of the weather, Elizabeth dressed and slipped quietly to the library. She intended to select a volume and return to her room, but she was distracted by the lightning skipping across the sky and turned instead to the window to watch the storm.

Darcy was displeased by the turn in the weather. Though spring rain was nearly always welcome for his crops, he had rather hoped it would hold off just one more day. As it had not, he adjusted his plans and sought out Georgiana and Lydia. He would need their assistance both in locating Elizabeth and in keeping Mary distracted long enough for him to achieve his purpose. He found them in the music room, and it was only after promising them each two new pieces of music and several lengths of ribbon that they would agree to assist him. They had begun their demands with three pieces of music and fabric enough for one new dress each. In his frustration with the girls, he briefly recalled being pleased when Georgiana had discovered she need not always be meek and compliant. Then he considered that he would have gladly purchased each girl a Season's worth of dresses and a new instrument if only he could have half an hour of uninterrupted time with Elizabeth.

When Darcy entered the library half an hour later, his irritation at having to resort to bribery in order to gain a private audience with his love vanished instantly at the vision before him. There, wrapped in a shawl and lit only by the occasional burst of lightning, sat Elizabeth. He watched her for several minutes before moving silently to stand behind her. "I have always loved the rain," he said quietly before placing a gentle hand on her shoulder.

She startled briefly but settled almost as fast then placed her hand atop his where it rested. She gave it a light squeeze and said, "As have I. It is"—she hesitated, then finished—"cleansing, as though the world will be made new with each drop that falls."

He dropped his head slightly to breathe in the scent of her hair. "Aye, that it is." They remained in their places for several minutes in silence before he spoke again, "I had intended to seek you out today."

She smiled and gently teased, "How would that be different from any other day, Mr Darcy?"

He moved then to stand in front of her, wanting to see her face—wanting her to see his. "It is different because today I wish to speak with you privately."

Elizabeth turned her face to his, seeming not to even breathe. "It would appear you have managed to do so."

"I had a plan, you know. I was going to walk with you to the bridge before taking your hand in mine. I even practised and wrote notes. I am much better with the written word, you see."

"Will you not tell me what you were going to say?" Elizabeth encouraged.

Darcy shook his head, "I cannot. I had a very pretty speech made, and then I saw you here and I knew."

"What did you know, sir?"

"I knew that there would never be words sufficient to my cause. I love you, Elizabeth. I have loved you for so long that I can no longer remember a time when my heart did not belong to you. I love you beyond all sense or reason. I loved you in Hertfordshire when you teased and tormented me with your dancing eyes and impertinent tongue. One moment you were just another lady, and the next I loved you so much it frightened me. To my eternal shame, I ran.

"It was my good fortune that Richard, unlike nearly everyone else of my acquaintance, has no fear in pointing out my failings. It was he who showed me my own arrogance and hubris, and when he was done, I could think only of returning to Hertfordshire to earn your love.

"When I learnt you had already been wed, I could not breathe, Elizabeth. I stood in your mother's parlour listening to her boast of her good sense and fortune, and I wanted to die. I wanted to rage against the injustice of it all. I could not understand how the world could simply continue on as if nothing so completely horrible had just come to pass. How could flowers bloom or birds sing in a world where you were forever beyond my reach?

"My heart ached when I saw you in Kent. You were still so strong and brave, still devoted to your family, and I loved you. You came to Pemberley, and my heart shouted that you were home, that you were where you belonged. I watched as this place began to heal you. I saw when the light returned to your eyes, and I loved you. I loved you at Ashford Lodge when you spun circles in the falling snow and enchanted my entire family, and I love you now."

He paused and dropped to his knees, taking both her hands in his before continuing.

"This is not what I had planned. You deserve flowers and romance and pretty words. I wanted that for you. But faced with you, faced with this consuming love, I find my plans are all for naught, and I can think only of persuading you to stay here with me for the rest of our lives.

"Elizabeth Bennet, keeper of my heart and possessor of my soul, will you marry me?"

She was silent as he confessed his love, the tears on her face the only outward sign of her feelings. At last, she whispered, "I wonder if anyone has ever been as happy as I am right now." Then the words fell from her lips, "Yes. Yes, a thousand times, yes!"

Darcy replied to her acceptance as sensibly and warmly as a man violently in love can be expected to do, and in her joy, Elizabeth laughed.

۞

May 14, 1814
Pemberley, Derbyshire

Dear Papa,

I am sending this letter in care of my dear Mr Darcy because I know, after my disastrous first match, that you will be cautious in giving your approval to him.

How can a daughter speak to her father of the man she wishes to marry? I love him, Papa. I love him with my soul. It is not his money, nor the security and respectability he can offer that I love. I would love him even if he were only a servant. I love the way he listens when I speak. I love the way he encourages my impertinence and seeks my opinion. I love the peace I feel when he enters a room. I love the way he looks to the needs of my sisters and his own. I love the way he cares for all those under his mantle of responsibility. He is a kind master, a good brother, and a most excellent man. He is reserved in the company of those he does not know, but I can find no fault in that. He loves me and he respects me. 'Tis more than I ever thought possible in a marriage partner.

I hope this letter gives you peace. If you find yourself in need of additional incentive, the library at Pemberley is astonishing, and I believe even you could quite lose yourself for days in its volumes. Mr Darcy bid me to invite you to come at any time and stay for as long as you like.

Your love-struck daughter,
Elizabeth

May 18, 1814, Longbourn

"What brings you here on this fine day, Mr Darcy?" Mr Bennet said by way of greeting.

Darcy clutched a letter in one hand, abusing the paper badly as he first clenched, then released his fist repeatedly. "I have come to ask after your daughter. Or rather, to ask if I might speak to you of your daughter."

"I am always happy to speak of my daughters, Mr Darcy.

What is it you wished to say?" Mr Bennet's eyes were alight with mischief.

"I wish to marry her, sir," Darcy blurted. "I wish to marry your daughter."

"Ah, I see. Well, Lydia is full young to be married. No matter that she has been out these two years at least. But, you young men will do as you wish, and she does have a lively disposition," Mr Bennet teased.

Darcy flushed. "It is not Miss Lydia's hand I seek,"

"No? Then Catherine perhaps? She is a lovely girl and certainly more retiring than her younger sister. Though, do not let her easy manner deceive you. My Catherine is a determined sort, but I suppose you already know this."

"I do, sir, but it is not Miss Catherine I wish to marry. I much prefer—"

"Mary! Of course! She is quite intelligent and easily a match for you. I daresay you will never lack for serious conversation with Mary as a wife." Mr Bennet's eyes were dancing with laughter.

"Elizabeth! It is Elizabeth I love and wish to marry!" Darcy exclaimed and thrust the now-wrinkled letter into Mr Bennet's hand

"Well, why did you not say so, lad?" Mr Bennet asked as he opened the letter. As he read, the laughter in his eyes gave way to open affection, and Darcy thought he saw tears gather in the older man's eyes. Mr Bennet set the letter aside and looked at the young man seated across from him. His teasing manner was quickly replaced with solemnity as he spoke. "Treat her well, Mr Darcy. She is precious to me."

"And to me as well, Mr Bennet—to me as well."

May 19, 1814
Longbourn, Hertfordshire

Dear Richard,

I have done it. I have asked my beloved Elizabeth to marry me, and she has agreed! I arrived in Hertfordshire only yesterday to seek her father's blessing, which I secured with only some little teasing on his part. He could not, of course, mistake the meaning of my appearance at his estate as there was no other reason for me to be in the neighbourhood.

Once we were established in his book room and I had stumbled through my reasons for seeking him out, the gentleman took great pleasure in tormenting me with suppositions of which of his daughters I might wish to marry and why each would be a good match. It was then I recalled the letter Elizabeth had given me for her father. I know not what she wrote, only that upon reading it Mr Bennet's face was graced with a soft smile, and he seemed no longer inclined to tease. Putting the missive aside, he merely looked at me and said, "Treat her well, Mr Darcy. She is precious to me." I assured him I could do naught else.

Tomorrow I travel to town to retrieve the settlement papers from my solicitor. I shall join your parents, brother, and his wife for a family meal before returning to Longbourn the following day. I shall share the news with your family at dinner. I anticipate they will be pleased and hope to apply to them for advice on managing any gossip surrounding our decision to marry before Elizabeth is officially out of mourning. I am depending upon your mother's assistance to ease Elizabeth's transition.

While I have complete confidence in my beloved, I know the support of your mother will do much to silence the worst of the gossips.

I plan to return directly to Pemberley from Longbourn, though I think I shall find it quite desolate. As we are now betrothed, Elizabeth thought—and I agreed—that it would be best if she were to remove with Miss Mary to stay at Grey Manor with the Bingleys and Miss Catherine. She will remain there with her sisters until we are wed. Though, if I am to be honest, Miss Mary is so diligent a chaperone, I was nearly unable to propose in any privacy and so would be in little danger of impropriety whilst she remained at Pemberley.

The banns are to be read in Kent and Derbyshire and we shall marry on June 21 from Pemberley. Mr Bennet had originally thought to join me on the journey north; however, he does not wish to arouse the suspicions of his wife. Though her means are certainly limited, we are both of the opinion that she could easily contrive to find her way to Pemberley or even Grey Manor if she were to learn of the wedding. As none of us wish for the company of Mrs Bennet, Mr Bennet will wait to make the journey.

If you find yourself in need of a respite, you and Lady Amelia are welcome to join me at Pemberley as soon as you find it convenient to do so. I have written to Lady Catherine and the Addisons inviting them to join us though I suspect it will not be possible as Anne is approaching her confinement, and I shall issue the same invitation to our Fitzwilliam relatives whilst I am in town. The presence of the Bennet sisters has quite nearly ruined my affection for solitude, and I find I prefer the halls of Pemberley when they are filled with the sounds of family.

Until then, I remain…
Your cousin,
Fitzwilliam Darcy

May 19, 1814
Grey Manor, Derbyshire

Dear Anne,

I write with news that I hope will bring you even a portion of the joy with which it is relayed. Fitzwilliam has asked me to be his wife, and I have accepted! He is even now in Hertfordshire seeking my father's blessing. We are to be married on June 21. My only regret is that you will not be present on that happiest of days.

I know you are wishing to learn more of the proposal and I shall keep you in suspense no longer. Once Mary and I arrived at Pemberley, I quickly resumed my habit of walking the grounds every morning and, when the weather and my sisters allowed, again in the late afternoon. It seemed no matter where my wandering feet might take me, I was nearly always joined at some time by Fitzwilliam. It was not long before Mary began the habit of walking out with me. She made a very diligent chaperone, and I hope one day to return the favour. Our little game continued for many weeks, and Fitzwilliam was careful to never ask more of me than I was prepared to give.

Five days past, I was forced to surrender my walk due to a thunderstorm, and I retreated to the library instead. Once again, Fitzwilliam found me. He told me later he had been forced to bribe our younger sisters to keep Mary occupied so she would not follow him to the library. We stayed there together, watching the storm for several minutes before your cousin stepped in front of me. He began awkwardly explaining what he had wished to do that day. Then he began to speak such words of devotion and love as to make me weep. He paused only long enough to kneel before me, grasp both my hands in his, and kiss them.

When he asked me to be his wife, I could at first barely whisper my reply, then the words came tumbling from my lips, "yes, yes, a thousand times yes." Once the words began, I was filled with such joy, such lightness, that I could not help but laugh. I wish I could describe for you the happiness that fairly radiated from his face or the way he was utterly transformed by the smile that graced his countenance. I have loved him for so long, Anne.

Though I could never acknowledge it before, I believe I have loved him almost from the beginning, and I had not dared to hope I could know such joy as for him to love me in return. I am truly the most fortunate of women.

Perhaps I should have allowed your cousin to relay our news, but I found I simply could not keep it to myself. He may tell the rest of his family, but I shall claim the rights of friendship in alerting you. Oh, I must thank you a thousand times for all you have done. If not for you and your family, I might never have survived my cousin and never would have found love with yours.

Your future cousin,
Elizabeth

ॐ

May 21, 1814
Longbourn, Hertfordshire

Dear Bingley,

I shall not bore you by repeating news you have already
heard from Elizabeth. Of my engagement, I can only ask
one question of you: How did you ever manage a
proposal under the watchful eye of Miss Mary? I
managed a private audience with Elizabeth only after
successfully bribing Georgiana and Miss Lydia with the
promise of music and ribbons in exchange for their
assistance. The girls then contrived to distract the eldest
Miss Bennet with a promise of new music. It was then but
the work of a moment to be relieved of our guardian's
presence. I shall never confess it to another, but I would
have gladly given more to gain those precious minutes.
As Miss Mary will soon be a resident of my household
and under my protection, I can only hope to one day
repay her kindness in the same fashion in which it was
rendered.

As you see from the direction on this letter, I remain at
Longbourn with Mr Bennet where I have been these past
few days, save a brief sojourn to town to retrieve the
settlement and deliver the happy news to my relations. In
the course of my visit, I have learnt some news that may
be of interest to your, and very soon to be my, family. It

seems Mrs Bennet will soon be without even the company of her sister Philips, who is now her only regular visitor. In recent months, word has begun to spread throughout Meryton of Mr Philips's role in effecting Elizabeth's marriage to Mr Collins, and as might be imagined, the news has been received in a rather poor light. With his clientele dwindling, Mr Philips has found himself obliged to sell his practice, and he will move south with his wife to Somerset. I am given to understand that Mrs Philips perceives herself as quite the victim in all this, blaming her husband and sister in equal measure while seeming to forget her earlier approval of the ill-fated match.

As to Mrs Bennet, I had the distinct misfortune to encounter that lady on my return from town. She was applying to her husband for more funds. I found her to be as unrepentant and vulgar as she has ever been, and I was perversely pleased to hear her lamentations as her request was denied. I think she at least suspects the reason for my presence as she began fawning over my person in a most ridiculous manner almost the moment she noticed me. She also suffers from the misapprehension that her daughter will now be in want of her advice. I am thankful I shall not have to endure her presence for the duration of my engagement as I believe I could not long be civil to the person responsible for Elizabeth's pain. As a precaution, I have sent word to Pemberley that Mrs Bennet is not to be admitted to the house under any circumstances in my absence.

I shall depart Longbourn for Pemberley on Monday and shall call at Grey Manor the day after I arrive to collect Georgiana and whichever of the Bennet sisters wishes to join her. If you are feeling generous, perhaps you might also allow me a few moments with my betrothed.

Your future brother,
Fitzwilliam Darcy

July 1, 1814
Pemberley, Derbyshire

Madam,
I have in my possession the ill-thought missive you presumed to send my wife on the occasion of our marriage, and I find myself obligated to respond on her behalf.

Not only were you not invited to the wedding, as you so politely mentioned, you will also find you will not be invited to any of our homes whilst I am living. I find it utterly reprehensible that you would disown your child for failing to produce an heir for that monster to whom you sold her, only to embrace her when it became evident her wealth and consequence might be of some benefit to yourself. It is your selfishness—your utter disdain for the feelings of others—that has convinced me you are the last person in the world I should be tempted to acknowledge. Can you possibly believe that any consideration would tempt me to tolerate the woman who has been the means of nearly destroying not only the happiness, but very nearly the life, of my beloved wife? I have every reason in the world to think ill of you. No motive can excuse the unjust and ungenerous part you played in orchestrating Elizabeth's disastrous marriage to Mr Collins. Nor can any excuse be made for your behaviour towards her since.

Elizabeth may one day wish to know you again, and though I can never encourage her in this, I shall not prevent her from doing so. Until she makes such a desire known to you, it is left to me to protect her, and I shall insist that every letter from your hand be consigned to flames before it even crosses her desk. And know this, Mrs Bennet—you will never have my good opinion, and I shall do everything in my power to assure you do not benefit in any material way from your daughter's newfound position.

Find a new home for your pleading and schemes. They are not welcome here.

Fitzwilliam Darcy

August 14, 1814
Pemberley, Derbyshire

Dear Papa,

Your letter was timed perfectly as we have only just returned from our wedding tour in Scotland. What a wild and beautiful country that is!

I know I may speak for my husband when I say of course you and Lydia must come to us as soon as may be and stay until you weary of our company. I shall hear no more of your protests regarding the newness of my marriage as an excuse to stay away. At the mention of your letter this morning, Georgiana proclaimed it to be absolutely necessary that she should see Lydia again, and Fitzwilliam informed me there is a game of chess yet to be completed between the two of you. So there you have it: you must come, for now it is both a matter of honour and an easy way of securing the happiness of your daughters.

For you, I know this need not be said, but if my mother should happen upon this letter I wish to be clear she is not included in the invitation.

Your happily married daughter,
Elizabeth

September 7, 1814
Pemberley, Derbyshire

Dear Uncle,

How can I thank you for your guidance and forbearance these past years? While I often turn to Richard for a brother's advice, I look to you when I am need of a father's wisdom.

I find myself more content than I ever dared hope I could be. Georgiana is increasingly lively, and she is refining the art of teasing even as she learns to be teased. Mary's improvement is remarkable. You did not know her before so you have nothing in way of comparison, but I assure you she has not always been as she is now. With the presence of my beloved Elizabeth, we have become a family, and life once again fills the halls of this home.

There is no sound more dear to me than that of Elizabeth's laughter, and I am privileged to hear it every day. Tell me, Uncle, who am I to deserve such joy?

Your nephew,
Fitzwilliam Darcy

November 26, 1814
Pemberley, Derbyshire

Dearest Jane,

Had anyone told me last year that I would now be so happily settled in a new life, I would have pronounced them ready for Bedlam. I now understand your words when you asked how anyone could be so happy. It is indeed far, far too much.

I am given to understand that I am now back in favour with Mama. I think it is not me but rather my husband's fortune that has won her over. I fear she shall not soon be in favour with either Mr Darcy or myself. Neither of us is quite willing to forgive her behaviour of the past year. Though I would not wish to be forever at odds, I do not see any possible way to return to civility.

But now to happier subjects. My dearest Fitzwilliam has made me whole. He has made me feel valued and loved. We do not always agree; indeed, with two such opinionated, out-spoken people in the house, such a thing would be nearly impossible. But when we disagree, there is no unkindness or disrespect between us. Even then, even when we are at odds, there is love.

Our family party is usually made up of Georgiana, Mary, and the two of us. We would welcome Lydia at any time, as I know you would. For now, she seems content to divide her time among three households. I believe she rather enjoys having our father's attentions for herself.

I am delighted to now inform you that you must be the first to wish me joy—we are to welcome another to our family in the spring. It is, perhaps, too early to share our news, but I find I cannot restrain myself. The newest Darcy is expected to make an appearance in late May or early June.

Dear, dear, Jane, how magnificently different is my life now from what I ever imagined. We do not do anything extraordinary. In fact, we are quite dull, I suspect. We read, we walk out together, the girls and I play the pianoforte, we talk, and we sometimes play cards. But the most astonishing thing, Jane, the most wonderful, delightful thing is that we laugh. Oh, Jane, how we laugh.

Your incandescently happy sister,
Elizabeth Darcy

EPILOGUE

July 12, 1820
Pemberley, Derbyshire

Dearest Mary,

I know you are anxious for news, and as our father is not likely to remember to write for some weeks, I shall not keep you in suspense. Papa and Fitzwilliam are safely returned to Pemberley. Papa is well settled, and to the surprise of none, he has established his place in both the library and the nursery. Bennet and Andrew are quite as much in love with him as ever, and I daresay it will be no small task to remind my children that they must share their grandfather whilst their cousins are visiting.

Fitzwilliam is quite confident that you and Mr Carson will do well at Longbourn, as is Papa. If he did not believe you both capable, he would not have bestowed the estate on you. I believe you love Longbourn the best of all of us, and I am so grateful you will continue to do so as its new mistress. We look forward to imposing on your hospitality as often as possible.

It is very good of Mr Carson to include a stop at Pemberley on your wedding trip. I only hope you are not too scandalised when you arrive. Papa says he will not wear mourning for his wife when amongst only his family. He has declared that he spent these past six years grieving the loss of the woman he thought to be his wife, and now he considers his mourning complete. I confess to following his example in this. Mama has been lost to me for many years, and her physical passing brought only release to my spirit. I did try, even to the very end. But Mama would do naught but cast blame at my feet, and I find I cannot be sorry such trials are at an end. I am done with grieving her loss.

If your visit comes as planned, we shall all be together in a few weeks' time. Poor Fitzwilliam—to have to endure all five Bennet sisters at once. At least now, he has brothers to share the experience. Georgiana is most interested in meeting your husband. She is recovering well from Henry's birth and expects to be fit to travel in good time to see you arrived. Of course, Jane and Charles will come with Charlie, Hannah, and Thomas. They live so near us as to make travel quite easy even with the children. Catherine and Stephen wish to come for several days now as it will be quite impossible for her to make the journey in a few more months.

Oh! I nearly forgot—Fitzwilliam has invited Lydia's betrothed at the time you are to be here! You will at last meet Lord Ashcroft. Could you ever have imagined our sister becoming Lady Ashcroft? I know I could not, and

Lydia tells me she had no more idea of becoming a Lady than she did of being the last of her sisters to marry. No matter how grand she becomes with her marriage, she will always be Lyddie to me.

There will be one more for you to meet as well. I believe your newest niece or nephew will arrive in just a few days. Bennet and Andrew have declared they wish for a sister, and as they do not wish for a brother at this time, any boy will have to be sent back from whence he came. I believe my dear husband also hopes for a girl this time. I wish only for the child to make itself known.

I must close now. The boys are begging for a story, and I feel very much in need of a walk. I cannot wait to see you, dear one!

Your affectionate sister,
Elizabeth Darcy

July 13, 1820

Mary,
Your sister is quite exhausted and has asked that I post this letter as she was not able to do so before our darling Marianne made her debut in this world. She has her mother's eyes.

Affectionately,
F.D.

November 26, 1841
Pemberley, Derbyshire

My Beloved Fitzwilliam,

As I do every year on this day, I am reflecting on how very fortunate I am to love and be loved by you. After all this time, I am still in awe of the love we share and the life we have made. I cannot imagine a better man, a better father for my children, or a better husband than I have found in you. You have been my protector, my lover, and my best friend, and I cherish all we have together. Together in these many years, we watched as our sisters fell in love and became wives and mothers. We wept as we mourned the loss of Lady Catherine, my father, and those little lives lost before they were begun. Together we trembled with fear and laughed with joy as we watched our children grow from tiny infants to bickering siblings and finally to brilliant adults. This year we have seen our dear Marianne become a wife and witnessed Andrew take over Summerton as its new master. I find it fitting that this day made us grandparents as Bennet and Lady Margaret became parents, and we welcomed the next generation of Darcys to Pemberley.

I have always considered this day to be an anniversary of sorts. It was on this day that we each made judgments and choices that would forever alter our lives. And while some might look upon the occasion with regret, I find I can only look on the date with fondness. It was that night we shared our first dance. It was the first time I felt the warmth of your hand through my glove, the first time I admired your form, the first time I truly wished for you to think well of me, and though I had not yet learnt, it was then that I began to love you.

I shall always treasure this date because, however twisted the road became, the twenty-sixth of November marked the beginning of a journey that led my heart to yours. I loved you then, I love you now, and I shall love you to the end of my days.

Your hopelessly besotted wife,
Elizabeth

November 26, 1841
Pemberley, Derbyshire

My dearest, loveliest Elizabeth,

Even as I write the words, I can see your curls bounce as you shake your head at them and I can hear your sweet voice decry their veracity. But I can attest you are still by far the handsomest woman of my acquaintance, and as you know that I abhor disguise of every sort, you must accept my word in this.

I was first struck by your beauty on that twenty-sixth of November so many years ago, and on our wedding day I thought you would never again be so beautiful as when you were standing at the altar with the light of the stained-glass windows dancing off your hair. I believed the same when I beheld your exhausted, joy-filled eyes after the birth of each of our children and again as each of them wed. I thought it once more today as I watched you hold our first grandson in your arms.

But your beauty is not only in your face and figure. It is in your strength. It is your grace in the face of trial and grief. Together we have experienced love and loss, and in each moment, you emerged triumphant. It was you who comforted Anne when she lost her mother, and you embraced our children when their hopes for another sibling continually ended in disappointment and grief. It was to you our sisters turned for guidance in navigating the treacherous waters of love, courtship, and mother-hood. And it is to your account I might credit my every happiness.

So on this thirtieth anniversary of our first dance and the first time I was overwhelmed by your presence, allow me to tell you again how ardently I admire and love you.

Forever thine, forever mine, forevermore,
Fitzwilliam

ABOUT THE AUTHOR

Kay Bea is an administrative assistant and Jane Austen lover living in Kansas City with her husband of 25 years, her mother-in-law, and her fur kids. She has written several short stories and drabbles on fanfiction.net as I Found My Mr. Darcy and on A Happy Assembly as MrsDarcy2032.

Kay grew up in Wyoming, enjoyed a two-year adventure in Maryland, and now calls Missouri home. When she isn't writing, Kay enjoys photography, cooking, and spending time with her adult children and three granddaughters.

This is Kay's debut publication. Her second book, *Love Unsought*, will be released in Summer 2020.

For more information about new releases, sales and promotions on books by Kay and other great authors, please visit www.QuillsAndQuartos.com.

ACKNOWLEDGMENTS

Â I started this story on a whim and could never have imagined it would end here, so thank you, Amy, Jan, Kristi and the team at Q&Q for taking a chance on me. There are so many people who helped along the way: Liz, who said she loved my voice; Jesse Jo, who waited for each new letter and was the first to get them in print; Heidi, who asked, Why don't you just do it?; my incredible husband, who dreams big and sacrificed sleep to listen to whatever new story plan I'd concocted; and Devika, who always wanted to know when I would be writing more. Thank you for pushing me, for believing in me, and for listening when it mattered.

Made in the USA
Monee, IL
01 March 2020